CHASING PAINTED SKIES

RYAN JO SUMMERS

Published by Satin Romance
An Imprint of Melange Books, LLC
White Bear Lake, MN 55110
www.satinromance.com

Published in the United States of America.

Cover Design by Caroline Andrus

CHAPTER
ONE

Raven Koynes moved the lace curtain aside and took a long look at the scene. Snow swirled like a large-scale version of a snow globe. The wind howled, rattling the aged windowpanes. She could not believe the severity of what forecasters had labeled a mild wind from the west. Despite the weather forecaster's continual assurances to the contrary, the winter snowstorm was continuing to grow. Right now, based on the amount of fresh white on the ground and the whitecaps slamming the rocky shore, she seriously wondered how worse it was going to get.

"So much for that mild wind from the west," she muttered. If this were what the forecasting experts called a mild wind, she would hate to see what they considered serious. Based on her experiences, this was promising to be a real snowstorm.

If a storm was coming her way, which she believed, she wanted to be someplace where she could see it properly. Her favorite place to be during a storm was at the top of the lighthouse tower, standing so close to feeling the cold touch of the glass on her nose and fingertips, and watching nature's furious onslaught. Alone at the top of the tower, with only the slightest bit of apprehension, did she witness nature's stormy symphony.

The excitement of seeing lightning as it sliced through the sky. The thunder boomed close enough to shake the tower's structure. Hailstones striking the roof and glass like pebbles tossed from heaven. She thrilled at the heavy rain falling, blurring her vision and then blending with the churning water below. The waves grew with increasing height, sometimes reaching over twenty and thirty feet during severe storms. Gradually, the storm would pass, leaving a few timid raindrops to settle and disappear on the water's surface. The whole scene never failed to leave her stunned.

Donning her lined jacket and cap, she pushed the front door open, ducking into the wind, and immediately the chill surrounded and crept down the back of her neck. As if forewarning the storm, scattered cold raindrops nipped at her. Making her way to the shore, sidestepping stones slick with fresh snow and jogging over the flatter sections of ground, she hoped she was wrong. The waves crashed into the shoreline around five to ten feet high. Surely, her guest wouldn't pick now to come out? Surely, he would wait on the mainland. Finding a solid footing on the worn rock, she hugged her jacket close against the biting chill, scanning the horizon, and wanting to be wrong.

This was going to be bad, she decided, meaning both the storm and the man. So, which one was going to reach her first?

She knew she could weather the storm until it blew over. It was the man who was bothering her more. Much more.

Sebastian Knight was a renowned photographer for some world-famous magazines. He also had several big glossy coffee-table books filled with his photos of exotic locations. Many of his pictures are displayed in prestigious galleries, and several have won elite awards. In short, Sebastian Knight was famous.

She knew all this because they were the selling points that had practically been shoved down her throat, leaving a bitter taste in their wake. Mr. Knight's publicist had wanted to send him to her home on Gull Island on Lake Superior's rugged shore to photograph its wild, natural, untamed beauty. That's how they referred to her slice of heaven when they politely inquired. And since the Coast Guard owned the island and the light station that was her home, she was powerless to prevent the request.

Her brother, Wren, a Coast Guard officer, had explained all of this to her. He begged her to be nice to Mr. Knight, let him snap his pictures, and then send him on his merry way. He had promised her the man would be gone in a couple of days. He assured her she'd barely notice he was even around.

Wren arranged for the publicist to send her a copy of one of Mr. Knight's books. Grudgingly, she read through it one evening, wanting to hate everything about the book. Between the thick covers were photos of frozen rivers, silent mountains cloaked in snow, and frozen icicles suspended in midair. There were photos of fields lying dormant under blankets of white, a snow-covered park bench, thick piles of snow covering quaint country bridges, a row of pine trees fringed in white lace, and many more within the pages of the book he simply called *Winters*.

Some were locations she recognized, such as winter over the Grand Canyon, sunny Palm Beach, across Maine, the Alaskan wilderness, and the Golden Gate Bridge. Others she referred to the subtitles to identify. Being not much older than her, it boggled her mind that one person could see so much of the world.

Thunder cracked, pulling Raven's wandering attention back to the gathering storm. And right now, this Mr. Knight was coming to take thousands of photos of her quiet island home, exploit them in his famous magazine and glossy books, and make tons of tourists want to come to her tranquil island. The wild, untamed beauty would soon be spoiled by thoughtless vacationers. Like homing pigeons, they would flock to Gull Island, and soon it would become part of the official Superior Lighthouse Touring Circuit.

Drawing her jacket tighter against the increasing winds, she nodded to the storm clouds and crashing waves, feeling some of the same fury building within her. The deal with Knight's people and the Coast Guard was airtight, Wren had assured her, so she needed to be civil. And she would be, to please her brother. But no one said she had to assist with his work. Tart satisfaction filled her with the thought of how she could subtly make his stay as unpleasant as possible, so much so that he might abandon the project and leave posthaste. She smiled, then laughed out loud as she imagined creative ways to be civil but uncooperative. Suddenly, she was eager to climb the tower and enjoy the mighty storm. Then she spotted the small dinghy bobbing on the water. Pausing, her heart sank at the realization she was not going to make it to the light tower.

Her jaw clenched in disgust, and then slow worry filled her, chasing away the earlier satisfaction. Following the boat's progress, she knew she had been right. It could only be the world-famous Sebastian Knight coming, riding the swelling waves like a cork in a bathtub.

Stupid, stupid, foolish man.

It would be a wonder if he did not crash upon the rocks first.

———

Sebastian fought the propeller's handle with one hand and tried to hold the camera steady enough with the other with a clenched jaw. If the waves slackened for a few seconds, he would have some shots of the cloud banks with the high swells behind them. The waves sloshed over the boat's edge. His pulse quickened with each deluge. Wonderful and wild, he thought, with a rush of excitement. Nature's fury as it gained momentum. What a powerful thing. He smiled, laughing into the raw energy swirling around him.

Another wave rocked the boat. He took the shot blindly, snapping a couple of pictures and hoping for the best. Quickly, he returned both hands to the task of getting safely to the house lit up in the distance. Beside the white clapboard two-story Cape Cod cottage, the stately alabaster light tower appeared as a welcome respite, beckoning him with its steady light. His arms ached with the continued effort of controlling the minuscule boat. The winds increased as he went further out on the water.

If they had expected this storm, why had they not given him a bigger, quicker boat? Surely, something heavier and faster would have been a better rental choice unless they had intended to drown both him and the boat. If so, they might succeed yet.

Riding the crest of the waves, he drew close to the shore. Building details bobbed into view. Straggly trees and seagrass whipped in the wind. He decided, with great satisfaction, that he was going to make it safely to land. He spotted numerous potential great photo opportunities welcoming him. For a moment, he debated whether to attempt using the camera for some shots approaching the shore and the light station. The dark swirling clouds framing the majestic tower would make a perfect shot.

Loosening his tight grip to remove his hand from the

propeller handle, thunder boomed, followed by a flash of light. A woman stood on the shoreline.

Abandoning any ideas of catching more pictures, Sebastian concentrated on guiding the tiny craft to the wooden dock. The wind whipped the woman's dark hair as she reached for the rope he held.

"Thanks." He offered a grateful smile as she secured the boat. He gathered his belongings. Thank goodness everything he owned was waterproof. "I wasn't sure I'd make it in before the storm hit. Looks like I just made it."

She cast him a wry look. One that took him aback momentarily. Standing, loaded with his equipment, he studied her. "I'm Sebastian Knight. Hopefully you were expecting me." He offered his hand.

"I was. I'm Raven Koynes," she said, though not taking his hand. "Come on inside before we get drenched." She reached instead for a couple of his cases.

Wordlessly, he handed over two lighter bags and followed as she led the way up the rocky path toward the house. The lights blazed within the structure, creating a sense of a warm and inviting home.

"Interesting last name you have," he said, keeping up with her. "Is it French or Irish, like as in a handful of pocket change?"

She turned just enough for him to catch a glimpse of her profile. He noted a wry, thin line pushing her lips upward.

"Something like that, except it is spelled K-O-Y-N-E-S."

"Okay, I'll remember that." He wasn't sure what to say. Her cool indifference was not what he had been expecting.

Thunder crashed around them as they hurried up the rocky trail. Reaching the house, Raven swung open the front door, rushing in. Sebastian crowded in behind her scant seconds before lightning streaked across the sky, opening with pouring rain.

"Wow, that was close." Sebastian pulled on the door, wrestling it away from the wind. Once the knob latched, he turned to the massive front room of an equally giant house before resting on Raven.

"You have a nice place here," he said. "Very nice and very large. Victorian?"

"Almost. Thank you. I like it."

"Don't you get lonely here, all this space, just by yourself?"

"I happen to like all this space and just myself, Mr. Knight."

Okay, point taken. For someone so pretty, he'd bet she had a spicy tongue when she wanted. Raven, the name suited her. Her long brown hair was as dark as a raven's wing. Her dark brown eyes shone with a light that made him wonder what she was thinking. She had a pretty, heart-shaped face and lips that begged to be kissed. Her height reached his shoulders.

Amethyst earrings swung at her ears, catching the glow from the massive stone fireplace. A rough-sawn wood beam spanned the length of the fireplace. Photographs in heavy wooden frames lined the beam, arranged on a lace runner. His gaze stayed fixed on the purple earrings.

A February baby, he mused, intrigued both by the sparkling mulberry stones and the woman who wore them.

She glanced at her wrist, then looked back at him again. "It's late. I bet you're hungry. I have stew heating on the stove. Would you like to get settled in and have something to eat, Mr. Knight?"

The way she made the offer made him think her heart wasn't in it. Professionally polite was the term that came to mind. He had been hoping for something more. Perhaps someone as excited about his photography as he was. Raven gave him the impression that if all his cases sank to the bottom of the lake, she'd be okay with that.

He cleared his throat, ready to try a different tactic.

"That sounds fine. I'd appreciate it. You can call me Sebastian if you like, Raven."

She ignored his words and approached the swirling staircase. "There are two sets of stairs in this house," she explained along the way. "This is the primary one, and the second is off the kitchen, toward the back of the house. There are four bathrooms and five bedrooms. I'm sure you will be comfortable during your stay."

"I'm sure I will be," he murmured in awe of the house. Arriving, twirling turrets and the sweeping porch fought for his attention in the storm's light. Inside, the papered walls, thick carpeting, and furnishings in a Victorian color scheme of black, maroon, and gold, all tastefully mixed with nautical motifs. Pictures of freighters and yachts shared equal wall space with Victorian ladies and children.

Raven pushed open a door. It gave a soft squeak of aged hinges. "Here is your suite." She moved away to give him space. He noted her excessive distance.

Stepping inside, he immediately caught the scent of pine coming from a glowing candle on the dresser. The wrought-iron, king-sized canopy bed was draped with thick, deep-red curtains and gold tasseled tiebacks. A walk-in closet promised he would have plenty of storage space, and he caught a glimpse of an en-suite bathroom with an ivory claw-foot tub. A wingback chair beside the crackling fire stocked with wood invited him to sit and relax. He set his bags and cases in two piles, one on the bed and one on the floor beside it.

"One of the nicest places I've stayed in a long time," he offered. Compared to some locations he shot at, he felt like he was in a palace. "So, if this was originally a lighthouse, why is it so large?"

Turning to face him, she licked her lips before answering.

He wondered if it was a nervous habit or just an unconscious action. Whichever it was, it only served to draw his attention to her lovely lips.

She set the cases he'd given her on the dresser, then turned enough to answer him.

"According to the Coast Guard, this place was first opened in 1876 and housed the light keeper, his wife, and their family of six children. Due to the location and the boats available at the time, they would find themselves isolated here for most of the winter. Space was important to store their provisions for the long winter and allowed space for the growing family."

Sebastian leaned against the wall, crossing his arms. How many times had she found herself isolated here alone? He considered asking, but decided against it, opting to focus solely on the property. For now. "Interesting. And all the outbuildings I noticed?"

"There is the tower, of course, which still operates today thanks to automation. There is the old barn, where the early families housed their cows and livestock they needed for survival, and a boathouse."

She went to the dresser to blow out the candle, pushing her long hair behind her ear. "Plus, the smaller buildings needed to operate the tower. One used to be an oil storage room, and the other was for something else."

"Something else?"

She shook her head, slowly turning back to him. "I don't recall what exactly at the moment. Does it matter?"

"No, not really, I guess. Do you care if I check them out later?"

She shrugged. "Whatever you want," she replied coolly. "I'll leave you to settle in, and you can come to the dining room when you're ready. The stew should be ready soon." She slipped from the room.

Puzzled, he watched her go. Just when she was starting to warm up a little, she cooled off. He liked her habit of licking her lips before she spoke. If she kept it up, he would be mighty tempted to kiss her yet. And, unless he was reading her entirely wrong, which was possible with her hot and cold personality, she would have a temper under that professional façade. He made it his business to successfully read people. So, if he kissed her, how much temper and rage would he get in return?

Amused by the possibility, he placed sweaters, Henley's, tees, and socks into the drawers, hung flannel shirts and jeans in the closet, not even putting a dent in the space that was offered. He lined up the cameras and other cases along the wall. The wrap-around turret window seat would offer a nice view. Kneeling on the seat, he leaned his head against the cool glass, feeling the chill against his cheek.

The view was better than nice. It was magnificent. Three windows rimmed the turret. The first one overlooked the distant rocky hills full of pine trees, while the second faced what had to be the boathouse Raven had mentioned, and the final window encompassed the mighty lake, still agitated by the churning storm, and the stately lighthouse tower.

Studying the wildness of the cold crashing waves, he could not suppress a shiver. Rain pelted the thick glass. Lightning slashed the dark sky with a brilliant flash. He jumped off the cushioned bench and prowled around the room to the other windows. Each one offered a different view of his location.

Snow-covered trees led into the wooded trails. Waves

and gnarled pine trees hemmed the long stretch of rocky shoreline. His rental boat, tied to the narrow boat dock, bobbed like a toy in a bathtub when the water drained out.

Clouds. Waves. His fingers twitched with anticipation at so many amazing photographic possibilities.

Oh, he was going to love this place.

———

He may be a fool, Raven decided as she descended the back stairs, but he was also handsome. Those emerald-green eyes could bewitch a tree trunk.

It seemed almost unfair to give such beautiful green eyes like that to a man and then add a charming smile and the silky head of short, dark hair. To complete the picture, he was tall, lean, muscular, and well built. And foolish, she added, lifting the lid from the stew. She stirred it, releasing the rich aromas into the room. He was lucky to have made it before the storm swamped his little boat.

She might not like him being underfoot, but there was no way she would miss noticing him. Wren was going to be very wrong in his prediction. Already, she was finding it hard to ignore his natural charm and manners, and he was unnerving her. Darn the Coast Guard for allowing him to come. Darn Wren for not fighting harder on her behalf.

Hearing her guest's footsteps on the stairs, surprisingly light for such a big man, she grabbed two bowls and quickly ladled stew into both. Carrying them to the dining room, she hoped he didn't notice her trembling hands as she placed them on opposite place mats on the long table.

"Dinner is ready. Seat yourself." She hastened back to the kitchen for their beverages.

Returning with a coffee carafe, she was startled to see him at the window, not seated at the table. He held the sheer, aged ivory curtain back, and his reflection in the glass looked somber, his brows puckered. Elsewhere, he remained alert, handsome, and every bit as irritatingly sexy as before.

"That's some storm whipping up out there," he said, glancing at her over his shoulder.

He caught her gazing, and her face heated. She hoped she wasn't so transparent that he could read her thoughts. *How embarrassing.* "It's a little early for a nor'easter, but anything is possible out here." Brushing her hair back, she crossed to the fireplace and added a fresh log, watching the sparks. His interested gaze seemed to match the heated sparks of the fire.

Darn Wren. This was not what she had been assured of. She closed her eyes and slowly inhaled, trying for composure.

"Aren't you worried about it?"

At his persistent voice, she opened her eyes. He'd fully turned from the window and watched her expectantly. He wasn't a particularly large man, probably average by normal measurements. However, aside from the physical attractiveness he'd been born with, there was a presence in him, an air or something invisible that refused to be ignored. Something almost magnetic.

Composure. One. Two. Three. Composure.

"Not really. I've been through storms here before. If the power goes out, there are plenty of candles and lots of wood for the fireplaces. There is an old wood-burning stove in the kitchen as well as the electric one."

"Seems you have it all covered. The stew smells good." Sitting, he moved a spoon through the thick broth, taking a sample bite.

She joined him, three chairs over, blowing on her spoonful before taking a bite.

"Um, this is good. What's in it?" he asked, eating another spoonful.

"Moose."

"Moose? Little dynamite, did you go out and shoot a wild moose for your dinner?"

She blinked at his question. *Little dynamite?* "What?"

"So, did you go out and bring this beast down yourself? Honestly, it would fit in with what I'm thinking you're capable of."

An involuntary smile curved her mouth, and her face warmed at his impulsive praise. Nice to know his opinion of her. "Hardly. My brother brought the meat from a moose hunt on the mainland. Seems they had a rogue bull that was causing trouble, so he joined the hunting party and shared the bounty with me." She hefted the spoon.

"I see. You and your brother must be close?"

She swallowed before answering his question. "We are. All four of us are close."

"Four? You have three siblings, and yet you choose to stay here in all this space and isolation by yourself?"

Lowering the spoon, she touched her fingers in turn. "Wren is the oldest, he's with the Coast Guard. I'm the next in line. Robin is my younger sister, and Lark is our baby brother. Four."

"Wren, Raven, Robin, and Lark. Your parents have something about birds?"

Her eyes narrowed and her back tightened, as did her fingers over the table's edge.

"You really want to have this conversation?"

He blinked. "I don't want to make you uncomfortable. It was a question, so I can better understand you."

Raven debated why he needed to understand her at all, considering his reason for being on her island. Then he cut her a smile, and resolve faded away. She uttered a sigh.

"They were ornithologists," she said quietly, a faint tremor in her voice.

"They were biologists who studied birds." He confirmed.

She couldn't hide her surprise that he recognized the technical term. He grinned at what she supposed was her startled expression.

"I have worked with a few while on bird-specific shoots," he explained. "So, what's with the 'were' part?"

She pushed her hair behind her ear and blinked back the burn in her eyes. "They were coming back from research in Brazil and their plane crashed."

"I'm sorry." He pushed the bowl away and moved his hand to her.

She wiped away the moisture in her eyes. *Darn tears. Every time.* "Me, too. But it was a long time ago." She did not want to feel his firm, warm hand on hers. She struggled to regain the cool detachment she had earlier. "Anyway, you asked."

"Okay. Point taken and note made. Be careful what I ask."

"That would be nice."

"Or at least how I ask."

She frowned. He really was such an irritating man. He might think that cute grin might disarm her, but she had no intention of falling under his charming spell.

Silence ruled following his statement. As they ate, she got lost in the contents of her bowl, and he was busy surveying the room like he planned to steal any treasures. What did he see in the room full of wall-length, glass-fronted China cabinets and dual chandeliers? Did he notice the hand-hooked carpets and ivy-designed table runner had seen better days? If so, he gave no indication.

"Hey, that moose stew was really good," he finally said,

after finishing a second bowl. Persistent, he trailed her into the kitchen. "I can honestly say I've never had moose before. So, would you like a hand cleaning up?"

Without waiting for her to turn him down, he rolled up his flannel sleeves and reached for the bottle of dish soap on the sink.

———

She arched her brow at his haste and determination to help. She would have shooed him away, but clearly, he was not one to be so easily chased off. Resigning herself to the fact he was going to remain underfoot, she scooped the last of the stew in a bowl to reheat for later and handed over the pot. Accepting it, he slid into the soapy bubbles and scrubbed, softly whistling a chirpy tune.

What did he think of her kitchen? Primitive? The water came from a small hand pump, not a regular kitchen faucet. Practical? A stone hearth dominated one wall, with space for two kettles to hang. Heat poured out from the small fire she had built earlier. Elegant? More glass-fronted cabinets held dishes and drinkware. Mother-of-pearl knobs and handles allowed access to endless rows of storage drawers and cubbyholes. Antique? There were few modern appliances, with only the cream-colored fridge/freezer combo standing among the nineteenth-century workhorses of the kitchen. Old? That it was, but she kept everything clean and working.

Whatever his thoughts, he kept them to himself. She went to the fireplace to fetch more hot water for the dishes, carefully pouring it around his hands in the sink.

Their gazes met. She froze, swallowing awkwardly.

"That is an interesting bracelet," she commented, noticing the wide, weathered leather band encircling his wrist. Stones of different colors lined the center of the bracelet, and a silver buckle held it in place. Despite herself, she stepped closer, drawn to the bracelet—and the man. She breathed in the scent of wild moose from his dinner, and a musky scent that seemed to naturally flow from him. "Aren't you worried about such a pretty piece of jewelry getting wet?"

"No, it gets wet a lot. It was a gift from a special friend years ago." He flicked his wrist, sending bubbles into the air. "Fact is, I couldn't take it off if I wanted to."

About to ask why, she changed her mind. Had it been from a girlfriend? A wife? *Where did those thoughts come from?* Startled, anxious for distance, she pulled a towel from the drawer, wet it from the small basin that rested on the counter, and washed down the counters. Soon, the kitchen was clean, and the dishes were dried and put away.

She hated to admit it, but they made a good team. His smug smile suggested he felt the same, and she was glad he refrained from pointing it out if that was indeed his thought.

"I'm going to check the weather one more time," she said, hands on her hips as she surveyed the room. Darn if they hadn't cleaned up quite well, and in good time. She was going to run out of things to do if he was going to remain constantly at her side or present in her path.

"Care if I come along?"

"Don't you have pictures to take or something?"

He smiled. "Not with the storm going on like it is. In fact, I can't go outside to explore until it passes and the weather clears. Right now, I really can't do much of anything except explore through this big house."

She cut him a frown. "Come on then. There's a radio in the living room."

Raven led him past the dining room, into the larger,

similar living room. She selected the velvet chair near the softly ticking Grandfather clock. She snapped on the radio and curled one leg under her.

Sebastian went to the stone fireplace, hands in his pockets, turned to where she could observe his profile as he faced both the edge of the fire and the window. He cast a strong, confident outline, illuminated by crackling firelight and backdropped by stormy darkness.

———

Two commercials from the radio filled the silence when Sebastian gave in to his curiosity and prowled the room. He studied the photos she had on display. One, clearly her brother from the Coast Guard, showed him in full uniform. He had the same thrust to the chin, same determined look, and identical eyes. Others showed what he assumed to be her younger siblings, also with the carbon copy features. And two of her parents, appearing much in love. He guessed one was from the early years of their marriage and the other closer to their fateful passing in the accident. The admiration in their eyes remained the same. How wonderful and how rare.

He lingered at a photo of what could only be from her graduation. A smile tugged at the corners of his mouth. She was delighted, an exhilarated sparkle in her eye, the look of someone ready to conquer the world. *Why is she living on this isolated chunk of rock?*

"Nightly weather report." The radio commentator's voice broke into his thoughts. "A mild storm has turned into an early-season nor'easter. Swells of five to seven feet have been reported, and winds in excess of fifty to sixty miles an hour. The Coast Guard has issued a ban on all craft for the remainder of today and into tomorrow. People are advised to stay where they are and remain inside until the storm passes. Repeating our top weather story..."

———

A turn of the knob, the radio silenced. Raven released a long breath as she gazed around the room. Great, just what she wanted to hear, she thought in exaggeration.

Sebastian stuffed his hands in his pockets. "So, what exactly does that mean?" He nodded toward the radio.

"That," she jabbed a finger at the radio, "means we'll be lucky if the power doesn't go out before the night is done and we'll be stuck inside for a while."

The power outage was something she could cope with. Being stuck inside with Sebastian Knight was another matter. The man was too charming, too handsome, too inquisitive, too...present.

A sound escaped his delectable mouth that was probably meant to be a laugh. Except she didn't see anything funny about their situation.

As the announcer had spoken, he'd inched closer to her, slowly stepping across the worn rug, until he stood a mere three feet away. She looked up at him as he glanced around the room and then back to her.

"Good thing it's such a big house. Guess it shows things could always be worse, right?"

His long arm swung around to remind her of the dimensions of the living room, and then he pointed upstairs and back toward the dining room and perhaps the kitchen beyond. He ended with a grin and a tilt of his head.

She failed to see how the size of the house mattered. He seemed determined to be in every room she was in. Rising to her feet, she went to the window facing the lake. Low moonlight shone through the heavy clouds, casting a dim glow over the rolling waves. The earlier rain had changed to snow, which was another indicator that this could be a serious storm.

Tops of trees bent low, almost touching the ground. Branches broke off, fluttering in the wind as if they were no more than feathers in a summer breeze. Lightning streaked through the sky, giving her enough light to notice something else.

"I hate to tell you this, but your boat is gone," she said softly.

Instantly, he was peering over her shoulder. "Gone? We left it tied to the dock."

She closed her eyes, inhaling his musky scent. Feeling his warm breath, laced with moose stew, on her cheeks, she forced herself to face the coolness of the glass, listening as the freezing rain slapped against the panes.

"I wonder if the storm pulled it loose," he said thoughtfully, casting his eyes up toward the sky and the revolving light beacon. "It could be anywhere by now." He moved to the fireplace, adding another log. It snapped and sparked.

"Don't worry. They have insurance for this kind of stuff. And besides, they should have known better to let you come out in such a storm with a small dinghy."

He cocked his head to one side, wearing a lopsided grin. "You know, I had considered that same thing. I mean about the storm and size of the boat. Well, at least I got all my equipment out of it."

"Yes, how lucky for you," she said quietly, wondering if losing his camera equipment would've spared her island home, or only postponed it. She also wondered how he would get off the island once his work was complete. Guess she would have to call the Guard, or better yet, call Wren, and have him send a boat.

A loud boom of thunder crashed overhead. Raven

involuntarily jumped. The room plunged into darkness, save only the flickering glow of the fireplace.

She silently cursed her luck. Like with most storms, she relished the solitude and chance they offered to step back from day-to-day routine. Without refrigeration and night-time lights, she was limited in daily choices. Normally, she found such periods peaceful and reflective.

"Um, you had mentioned this might happen," Sebastian said, his voice coming from the darkness. "Now what?"

Peaceful and reflective were not high on her list at the moment. With Sebastian at her elbow, she needed space to recoup. To breathe. To escape the way he filled her senses and her thoughts.

And now there was no way she could call Wren or the Guard until the power was restored. Which she knew would be a while. For a brief, passing second, she wished Gull Island offered cell phone reception. It never had, and she had no clue where she packed her phone away. But he doubtlessly had one. Wait until he learned it was useless on the island.

And there was no way she was going to stay in a dark room with Sebastian Knight.

"I don't know about you, but I'm going to bed," she announced. "Perhaps by morning things will be better." She spun, nearly running into his chest, and slipped around him to the side table along the stairs. She searched for the center drawer using her fingers, reached in and dug around, with-drawing two candles. She lit one using the fire and handed him the other one.

"Um...wouldn't flashlights be more practical?"

"Maybe." She thrust it at him until he was obligated to take his light. "However, wicks last longer than batteries. And if this outage goes for days, it's better to conserve flash-lights and rely on candles more."

"You have been through this a time or two."

His smile was warm, appreciative even, in the flickering glow of the fire. It stirred a warmth inside her, and she hastened to the stairs. "I have."

"In that case, goodnight, Miss Raven."

She paused at the landing and turned to his tall, slender silhouette in the fire's glow. Her palm sweated as she rubbed it on the smooth wooden knob.

"Mr. Knight, I feel I should warn you. If you hear someone prowling around in the dark, it's probably only Madeline. She's essentially harmless."

"Thank you for the heads-up. And who might Madeline be? A pet of yours?"

"No. The daughter of one of the early light keeper families who lived here. She never left."

His eyes widened as her words registered. "Like I said, she's more or less harmless."

CHAPTER
TWO

Sebastain stood by the fire, listening as Raven made her way upstairs before he dropped onto the velvet chair she had occupied. Inhaling, a unique mix of woods and fruits inundated his senses from the soft fabric.

Was she just baiting him with some ghost story? Well, he knew these old lighthouses had rich, long histories. It might be possible. Running a hand through his hair, he gazed at the fire. At least they would stay warm tonight. The chair was extremely comfortable. He might stay in the chair all night instead of going to the grand bedroom she prepared.

He grinned. Why had she offered him such a nice room when he had the distinct feeling she did not want him around? Surely, there must be another room less grand and fancy she could have stuffed him in. Or was she naturally hospitable, whether she cared for the guest or not?

He raked a hand through his hair, blowing out a breath. As a boy, he enjoyed reading detective novels. He'd even briefly considered a career as a police detective until he was bitten by what he called nature's shutterbug. But thinking of Raven now, he was ready to jump headfirst into her mystery, as he had fallen into detective novels from his youth. Determination gripped him. Just as he always had to read on to discover who killed the victim years ago, he had to plunge ahead and learn all there was about Raven Koynes.

———

If Madeline didn't scare her guest away, Raven didn't know what would. And it was true enough. She'd run into the girl plenty of times, and the teen seemed nice enough. For a ghost. But where did she expect Mr. Knight to run to if he was the type to be scared away by ghosts? Thanks to this ill-timed storm and the tiny rental boat, now lost to the waves, he was pretty much stranded on the island.

Setting the candle in its cradle on the dresser, she undressed and pulled on a nightshirt. She stepped to the dry washstand and poured a small amount of water from the pitcher into the bowl. She grinned at her reflection in the mirror, flickering in the candlelight.

Sebastian Knight was going to think he stepped back in time once he reached his room. Yes, true, the whole house retained the Victorian-era of its heyday, with only minimal upgrades as the Coast Guard deemed necessary. Perhaps the bedrooms retained the most vintage charm. This was never more apparent than when the power went out, and after dark.

She poured more tepid water from the ceramic pitcher into the water basin to brush her teeth. Night rituals complete, she could climb into bed. She hated to read by candlelight, as it usually caused too much strain on her eyes. She'd wait for the power to come back on before getting back into the book she found left behind from centuries before. She found the Victorian book in the living room.

She pounded her pillow into the preferred shape, slid

onto the mattress, and pulled the quilt to her chin, with thoughts brimming of Sebastian Knight. If she explained her reasons for not wanting the pictures taken, would he understand? He seemed quite reasonable and sensible. Would he agree to cancel the contract and leave empty-handed? She could point him to other untamed and beautiful areas around the lake that were not so close to her. Some were already national parks and were just as wild.

Perhaps, in the morning, she would mention it to him, see if she could get him to look at this intelligently. Smiling, she fell asleep, listening to the rain pounding the windows outside.

———

"Okay, so tell me about this keeper's daughter," Sebastian requested the next day when he joined her for breakfast in the kitchen. "This Madeline."

"Did she visit you last night?" Raven glanced up from where she was lighting the wood stove. From the looks of him, he must have slept in his clothes. She never heard him come upstairs. His rumpled hair, short as it was, looked entirely too cute. *Darn him.* Heat licked her fingers. She jerked her hand away from the flame.

"No, not that I noticed anyway." He scrubbed his jaw along the rough bristle. "I fell asleep in the chair and never heard anything until you started thumping around the kitchen just now. I figured you were a safer risk than she might be."

"Like I said last night, she was the daughter of one of the early families here. She died when she was somewhere between fourteen and seventeen. The written records differ. Her spirit never left the house." Raven snagged two pans from the upper copper rack and moved to the sideboard. "I see her from time to time." She shrugged nonchalantly.

He scrubbed his jaw again. "Okay, fair enough. No more Madeline questions. So, how do you suggest I get a shower and shave today?"

Darn, she kind of liked that rough look of the stubble on his chin. Good thing he wanted to shave it off. He had plenty of sex appeal already. Too much, in her opinion.

"There are jugs of water stored upstairs and in all the bathrooms. Enough for a quick bird bath and a shave."

"Seems you are quite adept at roughing it," he commented, as she pulled a burlap bag of bacon from the sideboard and sliced several pieces. Counting, she dropped them in the frying pan, where they soon sizzled. The scent of hickory filled the room.

"I've learned to be. There are a few drawbacks to no power." She grabbed four potatoes from the wooden bin and started scrubbing them.

He arched a brow. "There are? None I've noticed so far. Such as?"

"We can't use the automatic coffee maker. I'll have to put the old granite one on to boil. No eggs this morning either. I don't want to open the fridge if I can help it. Hope you don't require milk for your coffee."

He sliced her a warm smile, and her hand slipped, the knife close to slicing her. "I can rough it a little bit too," he assured her softly.

Turning away, she nodded and quickly set the knife aside. "Breakfast should be done by the time you finish cleaning up."

He gave a small laugh. "Okay, I can take your not-so-subtle hint."

Later, after a hearty breakfast of ham, hash browns, biscuits, and boiled coffee, she shooed him outside while she cleaned up the kitchen. She stood at the window watching him study the water's edge. He stepped carefully among the fresh patches of snow on the rocks. He hopped from snowy rock to rock, sure-footed like a billy goat and observant like a big cat on the hunt.

It was absolutely amazing how he could miss so little, at least to her observations, and be so lithe on the slippery shore. It really seemed unfair.

She rested her palms on the counter, fingers gripping the wash rag, as she watched him bopping his head around like he was at a music concert. At least the worst of the storm was past them, so he could get outside and do what he came for—photography. Except she had no opportunity to ask him not to take his pictures.

———

Sebastian surveyed the grounds. The opportunities here far exceeded his expectations. Once he brought his cameras downstairs, he was going to capture some great shots. First, he wanted to study the lay of the land, get a feel for the mood of the area, gain insight of the clouds, and breathe in the refreshing, cold air. He wanted to experience the still, moody winds that followed in the wake of last night's storm. Truth be told, he also needed a little breathing space away from his lovely hostess.

Seagulls, for which the island was surely named, dipped and called overhead, scanning the shore and rocks for edible debris from the storm. Finding a fish or something else dead, several descended upon it. Wings flapped as they chased each other away, or they snatched a quick bite before taking to the air again. Amused, he observed them for a while before moving further along the shoreline. Nothing was safe from his photographer's eye. He noticed every fluttering leaf, every wave that crashed upon the rocks, each passing bird, and each twinkling droplet of rain left by yesterday's rains. The bits of snow added to the pristine scene.

Larger patches of white show blanketed areas heading into the island's wild interior, deeper away from the water. Cold winds blowing down from the hills forced him to pull his collar a little higher. How soon would fluffy snow cover the entire island?

Picking his way carefully among the rocks, a chunk of submerged wood caught his eye. Stripes of white and blue, his heart sank at the realization of what it was. Or at least what was left of it. His rented dinghy, now broken and useless, lay smashed on the rocks. Great. Hopefully, Raven knew of another way for him to get off the island when he was ready. Surely, she had some means, a boat perhaps, to go to the mainland if she wanted. Snapping his fingers, he strode off to check out the boathouse.

Empty and deserted except for some birds he'd spooked when he hauled the heavy door open. They flew away through an open window high in the rafters at his approach, dust falling in their wake. Water lapped softly against the wooden dock.

Interesting. Raven had no car because there was nowhere to drive on the island. The landscape was hilly, wooded, and rough. She had no plane, as there was no length of land long or smooth enough for a strip. And she had no boat. Interesting.

She was something all right. Like those old detective books, she teased and tempted him to search for more clues to solve the mystery. The only difference he could tell was she had a fiery temper, warning him to go easy. Her calm confidence also intrigued him. If he had to describe her in one word, unruffled would be his choice.

———

"I found my boat," Sebastian announced as he entered the kitchen. "It's smashed on the rocks a few dozen feet from the pier." He straddled a chair while watching Raven pound two slabs of meat. "More moose?"

"I was certain your boat was history." She briefly peeked at him over her work.

"I noticed there wasn't another boat around. So, how do you get off the island when you want to?"

"I don't." She kept pounding the meat.

"Come on, surely you must want to get away once in a while. Go shopping once a month or something? You don't even have a car."

"I do have a car. Just not here."

"You live somewhere else? A place with a car?"

"No. I live here for now." There was no mistaking the keen interest in his tone. It was now or never. She paused, setting the meat pounder aside and taking a deep breath. "Look, Sebastian, there is a good reason why I like to stay here alone and don't go to the mainland."

"Okay, what is it?"

"It's hard to explain. But it is one of the reasons why I am...hesitant to have you come and take pictures."

He shrugged. "What's the harm in a few pretty pictures?"

"The pictures themselves, none. It's what is going to happen afterward." She wiped her hands on a towel.

"Which is?" He leaned into the chair's back, moving closer to her. Her heart skipped, hoping he was at least partially taking her explanation seriously.

"You know what happens when your pictures go into books and people see them," she pointed out. "I don't want that happening to Gull Island. This place is my home, and I don't want it to be filled with nosey, loud, and destructive tourists."

"Well, Raven, I don't know what to say. To be honest, that was not what I was expecting." Raking a hand through his hair, he blew out a breath. "I can't stop the wheels of motion now. There is too much riding on this project to just abandon it."

"Of course." She declared flatly.

"Now wait a second. If you were so against this project, why was it approved?"

She whirled, throwing the towel to the counter. "I had nothing to do with approving it," she declared. "It was completely decided upon by the Coast Guard. They still own the island and the light station."

His gaze drifted to where a few photos were displayed on the wall above the stove. Her gaze flickered over and returned to her work. She watched him under her lowered lids. His gaze wavered from her to the family photos over the stove and back to her. The longer she watched him watch her, she silently questioned how much he really understood the power of photos.

Unlike the generic vintage paintings and pictures, these were personal. Matted and framed, they were of her, her brothers, and their parents. They were happy times when they were all still a family. Could he see how important her pictures were, a connection to people she loved, and some she'd never see again? Could he tie it to how his photos could impact others too? This time to come to her home.

"Why are you here, Raven?" he asked quietly. "What did you leave behind to come hide out here?"

She wasn't expecting that. Her head shot up and she narrowed her eyes. Her breath hitched. "What makes you think I'm hiding out? What I left or did not leave is none of your business."

Sebastian Knight was a little too perceptive. Enough to unnerve her.

"So why—"

She held up a hand. "I live here now for reasons you don't need to know. I do not want pushy tourists overrunning my home like weeds any more than you would like them running amok through your house. That is all you need to understand."

Spinning on her heel, she marched from the room.

———

Shocked by her angry outburst, he watched her exit. Her steps pounded on the old wood flooring as she walked outside, closing the front door with a firm sound.

He liked how she stumbled on his name, as if it were difficult to use his name. She would probably be more comfortable calling him Mr. Knight. She seemed to like that emotional distance between them. Initially, he'd been unable to stop himself from being drawn into the explanation, awkward as it was. Certainly not what he expected to hear, but it clarified why he felt she didn't want him around. He took heart in that it wasn't him personally so much as what she thought his work would cause.

It all clicked now. Her brother, in his full uniform with numerous stripes and ribbons in the photo, must be a high-ranking officer who arranged for her to rent the area. But legally, she was only a tenant.

Eying the pieces of meat on the cutting board, whatever they were since she never answered him, he stood and pounded them a few times. Satisfied they were at least a little thinner than before, he placed them in a nearby bag of marinade she had prepared and left the bag of meat on the counter. Finished, he went to find her.

She might be angry, but he felt more compelled to draw her out. Like a bumblebee annoyed at someone near its flowers. Most folks would stay away from that situation, but it had never been his style. Smiling, he wondered how much punch her sting could really have.

———

Knees curled to her chest, gazing at the wind-tossed waves and soaring seagulls, Raven thoughtfully chewed her bottom lip. She tried her best to explain her reluctance. Obviously, he was either powerless or as reluctant to stop photographing. But which? No doubt he had people to answer to and would have some serious explaining to do if suddenly, he announced to them that he wanted to abandon the project, shred the contract, and move on.

Of course, he was a world-renowned photographer and all that stuff, with awards galore, so he undoubtedly had some influence with his superiors. Enough to call some shots when he wanted to, she would bet. If he wanted to.

And what was with all the questions? He never ceased to ask questions. How would he like it if she badgered him with endless questions every time he turned around?

Usually, the view from the porch gazebo could lighten her darker moods, yet right now, it failed miserably. Maybe she should go into the tower and watch the world from the widow's walk. It had been a while since she had been there. The view might give her a new outlook.

She wrapped her arms around her waist to ward against the cold while she strolled to the light tower. Halfway up the spiral stairway, she glanced through one of the random windows strategically placed along the tower's stone and spotted Sebastian crossing the rocky ground. Heading her way, of course. She blew out her breath. It turned to frost in the air. The man may be attractive as a Roman statue, but he was irritating as a horde of mosquitoes. She huffed another breath.

Quickening her pace, she finished the climb and stepped into the winds, high up on the railed walkway. Her hair whipped wildly in front of her face until she turned into the wind and gripped the iron rail. Off in the distance, the mainland's rocky shoreline with sheer cliffs and tree-covered bluffs was visible. It was a matter of time before he joined her.

Minutes later, his deep voice broke her silence. "I'm sorry," he said softly. The wind took his apology away. But she heard it.

He wrapped his hands around the railing to stand beside her, glanced at the water, and back to settle on her face. Wind swirled, whipping her hair around, so she had to peek at him through the blowing tresses. The wind seemed as unsettled as she was. West to east, north to south.

"I didn't mean to make light of your concerns or ask you a bunch of nosy questions."

A trace of a smile played on her lips, vanishing quickly. Yes, she felt the wind's indecision. Mr. Knight drove her crazy, but his sincerity softened something inside her.

"It's quite a view you have up here."

"I like it."

"Do you come up here often?"

She remained silent. The badgering questions just never ended.

"You don't like all my questions, do you?" he asked suddenly, stepping back from the rail. He still held his top grip but put a distance between them.

Startled, she turned to him, lips parted. How had he known? And why did the small distance instantly concern her? They were on the widow's walk. Space was limited, but why was a distance of two feet suddenly something to notice? Back to his question as he waited for her response.

"Good guess. Or have others indicated you asked too many questions?"

Chuckling, he looked at the endless repetition of the waves. "Both actually. But with you, it was mostly just a pretty good guess. Sorry I bother you with my questions. I'm just naturally curious. Must be what makes me good at what I do."

She shrugged, seeing a connection but not really caring at that moment. Instead, she ventured a question of her own. "So, isn't there any way you can abandon this project? At least here at Gull Island? I can point you to lots of rugged and wild places that would look just as nice in a book."

He shook his head. "I bet you can. There must be dozens of pristine spots like this around these big lakes. But for some reason, my people want this island. Don't ask me why. I didn't come up with it, and I'm just doing what I am told."

"You do that often, do you?" He didn't seem like the type for mindless obedience.

He laughed. "I never used to, but I am learning it helps keep the peace."

"Keep the peace?"

"Peace in my life. I learned I get a lot less grief when I just shut up and go where I am told to go and do what I am supposed to do."

That did not fit the character she had seen so far. "Hmm, I bet there is a story or two in there."

"There is." He nodded. "I wasn't always the sensible person you see before you. Once upon a time, I was rash and impetuous. But that is a story for someplace else."

"Heights don't bother you, do they?" Personally, she

loved high places. It's one of the reasons why she loved the widow's walk on the tower.

"Only when I am up high with someone who I don't think cares for me very much. Then they tend to make me nervous." He delivered a tentative smile. "Plus, it's windy up here."

Yes, they both could have worn thicker coats. Okay, he won this round. "We can go down to the gazebo, and you can tell me your story," she offered. "It's sheltered from the worst of the wind."

He smiled, extending his hand. "Deal. But don't have high expectations. It's not that fascinating of a story, really."

Taking his hand, she gave it a gentle pump. "Let me be the judge of its quality."

———

Soon they were seated at the gazebo, knee to knee. Raven clasped her hands together on her lap, waiting expectedly. She lifted an eyebrow. He fiddled with the bracelet on his wrist, then began.

"Well, I've always wanted to be a photographer. When I was just a kid, my parents bought me an instant camera and I was hooked within ten minutes in the backyard." He exposed a guilty smile. "My parents spoiled me since I'm an only child. I took photography in high school and gradu-ated with a scholarship to college for advanced photography. I worked my way up the ranks to get where I am now, but believe me, most of my success came as a surprise to me."

"How so?"

"I just wanted to chase the painted skies, shoot the shots, and capture the world on film. I never thought about books and awards and galleries."

"Chase the painted skies?"

34

He stretched an arm to the horizon. "My name for the sky at sunset. When the sun sets, when it's setting, the rays paint the sky with beautiful brushstrokes like on a canvas. I've seen it over the oceans, over the deserts, over the plains of Africa, and over the tundra of Antarctica. It's always my favorite scene and always leaves me breathless. It's the only name I could think of to adequately describe all those colors chasing each other across the sky, painting the horizon with shades from nature's vivid palette."

Goosebumps broke out on her arms. His vivid imagery gave her imagination wings. "No wonder you are so highly awarded."

"It's the clouds that make the sunset, you know," he continued, dropping his voice as though sharing a high-value secret.

"The rainbows of colors are endless. Different all the time, each night. Depending on how the clouds might be any given night, you never know what you might see."

"So where does the learning to keep the peace come in?"

He fingered his leather bracelet, his face an expression of thoughtfulness and reminiscence. "Well, it was about fifteen years ago, when I was first starting out with the group I'm with now. I had been a lone photographer up until then and had not yet figured out how to work well with others."

She returned his playful grin, getting into his story. "I can just see you acting impetuously." Boy, could she ever.

"Ah, I was so much worse back then." He wiggled a finger at her. "So, I was on one of my earlier assignments with them, out west to shoot some shots of this rare lizard. I was up on a canyon cliff, spotted a pretty one slithering across a rock, and leaned over for a better view. I slipped and fell, a *very* long way down to the canyon floor."

Her hand covered her throat, and her lips parted in horror as she gasped. Images burning into her mind.

"The fall probably should have killed me, but guess I got lucky. I don't know how long I lay there all smashed up. I eventually woke in the hut of some Native Americans who had found me. They used their medicine and somehow healed all the broken stuff inside me. It took months, but I finally recovered."

She swallowed, hand over her racing heart. "You were very lucky."

He nodded. "Yes, I was."

"Weren't your parents or employers, or anyone, trying to find you all that time?" *A girlfriend? Where did that idea pop in from?*

"Sure they were. All of them were. Except the tribe was well secluded. They were impossible to find unless you knew where to look. And no one expected me to be with them. I was supposed to be just photographing lizards in the desert."

"So what happened?" His story was so captivating that she wanted more.

"I stayed with them for many months, about eight or nine, I think. I learned a lot from them. And the medicine man gave me this bracelet as a gift before I left them." He extended his arm, holding back the sleeve to expose his wrist with the leather band and stone detailing. "Each stone has a specific purpose and a message. Loosely translated, it means to chase the painted skies but use some common sense too. He buckled it on and sealed it with magic, and I've never taken it off."

Raven felt her face pucker, like when she tasted lemonade. *Magic?* "You don't actually believe that, do you? Magic?"

He cocked his head. "Something healed me when I should, by all rights, be dead."

"I don't doubt they had good medicine, better than

most modern-day doctors. But magic? That was a bit much."

He shrugged. "You have a pet ghost."

"Not the same. Madeline is not a pet, but someone who once lived here. And there is a chasm of differences between ghosts and magic."

"I'll concede to that. They are different."

"Good." Raven glanced at the sweep of the light grazing the ground. "Okay, where does the keeping the peace part come in?"

"Oh, once I made it back to civilization, after being gone the better part of a year, I heard a few lectures. A bunch of them actually." He exposed that crooked grin again. "I finally learned it was easier to just do what I am told and shut up, don't take reckless risks, and all that sensible stuff. It keeps my life much more peaceful."

"So that's why you can't suggest to your boss to find someone else's island to photograph? Because it would not be sensible?"

"Because it would upset my peaceful existence with them," he modified. "Actually, there is more to it than just that. It's contract stuff too. You know, legal stuff I can and can't do."

"Like falling off cliffs while taking pictures of lizards?" And preserving the tranquility of her island home.

He laughed. "Yes, stuff like that. Actually, they did write a special paragraph into our contract regarding cliffs and taking careless chances. No kidding."

Raven slapped her hands to her knees, slowly rising. She didn't doubt the special paragraph. His employers probably had their hands full with him. "That was indeed a fascinating story. Your eyes sparkle, your voice catches, and you lean into the story. It's hard not to feel your passion and get caught up in it too. You tell it very well. Expectations fulfilled. But now, if you will excuse me, I think I'll go finish preparing our meal."

––––––

Sebastian let his fingers return to the bracelet as she strolled towards the house. The wild waves garnered his attention. So did the revolving sweep of the beacon's light over the waves. Rhythmic, relaxing.

Yes, it was a fascinating story, but by no means complete. He'd left out the most interesting part. The best part. The magic she scoffed at, attached to the stones fixed on the bracelet, was what allowed him to do what he did.

He was serious when he said he'd seen sunsets in the deserts, the oceans, Africa, and the Antarctic. Except he'd seen most of them in a different form.

To best appreciate nature at her finest, sometimes he had to become one with nature, so he could better capture her on film. He climbed the Rocky Mountains as a goat, swam the Atlantic and Pacific oceans as a dolphin. He had run the unsettled western lands as a mustang, feeling the hard desert floor under his pounding hooves and the freedom of the wild wind whipping through his mane. He'd soared through the skies as an eagle chasing the painted colors. He'd watched the sizzling Northern Lights as a polar bear. He'd swung through several jungles as a monkey in different countries and continents. And he'd prowled the rugged Serengeti as a ferocious lion.

How would Raven react if she knew he was a shapeshifter?

CHAPTER
THREE

"That's another great meal you made, Raven," Sebastian praised, patting his belly. "So what was the meat you marinated? Could it have been more moose? Elk? Something gamier like oh, say, beaver?"

"Beef. Hereford steer raised a few hours south of here."

He stood, gathering his plate and silverware. His brows puckered, and his lips pulled into a pout. Disappointment suddenly made him look like a schoolboy being told there'd be no dessert after dinner.

"Just plain cow?"

What had he been expecting? "I'll clean up." Raven jumped from her chair and reached for his stuff.

"All right then," he said. "Guess I'll take a walk since you don't need my help."

Raven heard Sebastian go upstairs for a few minutes, and then she heard the front door close. Alone at last, glad for the peace, she attacked each dish with renewed energy.

The man bothered her entirely too much, raising emotions she had thought were either erased or buried. Yet here they were, knocking at her mind's door, reminding her of memories forgotten. Memories she wanted to stay forgotten or lost.

The dishes completed, counters and table wiped down, she poured a cup of boiling coffee into a mug. Dressed for the outdoors, she headed for the gazebo on the porch.

The music drifting softly on the evening breezes stopped her. Following the sound, bathed in twilight and a glow from an oil lantern, Sebastian stood in the gazebo. He was the picture of concentration in the shadow of the light. Strapped around his neck was a golden saxophone and his fingers moved lightly over the keys. The sound hypnotized Raven. Leaning against the porch railing, her fingers cradled the mug.

He played a few chords, stopping and scribbling in a black notebook with a stubby pencil, only to resume the music again. The sax glinted in the light of the lantern. Rich and wonderful, soulful and almost haunting, the music held her.

Sebastian's fingers lifted effortlessly on the instrument, like a familiar friend. She imagined those long fingers gliding across her skin. A heat grew inside her, turning into rolling waves.

Time ceased. Fragment by fragment, the cold, hard pieces inside her melted away, yielding. She vowed never to fall for another man, to never love again. To refrain from becoming involved or to trust. But Sebastian Knight's lilting strands, artfully and slowly, slipped loose the knots of her heart, making her lose sight of those important vows.

If she were smart, she would leave now. Stop listening, quit watching his face in the twilight's glow, and walk away. Better yet, run away. Go anywhere. Someplace she could not hear or see him. So why couldn't she? Why did the silky strands of his music hold her heart captive? She'd never particularly cared for sax music or any music before. Most of it was okay, but she preferred silence. Why did this beautiful and poignant sound draw her in? Why did it untie those knots of resolution in her heart and mind? How did he awaken a desire within her that she thought was forever gone?

Trembling, she forced herself to move. Slowly, she retreated and returned inside the house. She sat alone on the balcony of her bedroom in the deepening twilight and bowed her head. Tears slid down her cheeks.

———

The song was shaping up nicely. Sebastian jotted down a few more notes in the worn notebook. Maybe he'd have it finished by the time he left the island. Who knew when that would be. Or whenever power would be restored. Raven had assured him there was no cell phone service on the best days, and the phone on the wall would not work until the power came back on. She also said her brother would not send anyone to check on her right away, as the Coast Guard was always busy after a storm like this one. Wren seemed confident she would be sensible and alright until he could spare a boat to come to the island.

Personally, he thought that was a bit selfish of the brother, but maybe that was just him. If he had a sister, capable or not, he'd never leave her alone way the heck out here and not make sure she had the means to communicate with the outside world at all times and check on her frequently. But they seemed pretty close, so maybe it was the brother respecting her wishes. He grinned. She could be a prickly little thing. Maybe her brother had been poked enough by her sharp spines to know when to back off.

Well, it was what it was, and their arrangement was between them. She seemed okay with her situation on the island. So, what about her other situation? The one where she had a car somewhere else?

The more he thought about it, the less anxious he was to leave Gull Island. Even without the added benefit of its natural beauty and charm, he felt pulled to capture on film, there was also the natural beauty and a buried charm to Raven Koynes. With some time and patience, and the right keys, he felt he could unlock that charm. He just had to endure a few more pokes from her prickly spines first.

He admired her confidence. Almost stately, and a little bit annoying. Perhaps that was how her brother felt.

Shifting his thoughts back to the song, he reviewed his notes. He liked the melody and the lyrics. It was a hobby of his, songwriting and playing the sax. He also played guitar, but the sax was more portable when he was traveling. Plus, he liked the saxophone better, being jazzier. He'd once gotten into a sold-out jazz symphony by shapeshifting into a bird and flying through an open back door and landing on the rafters above the musicians. It proved to be one of the best musical events he had attended, complete with his own bird's-eye view of the event.

Smiling at the memory, he picked up the pencil again, tapping his foot on the wooden floor. He may not be the best musician around, but he enjoyed what he did and how the finished product sounded. He preferred to think that a few others around him usually did too.

———

Still no power, Raven determined as she awoke the next morning. The sun shone through her windows, but the screen of her alarm clock was blank, with no red numbers to glow with the time. The salt lamp on her dresser also failed to glow its reassuring soft light.

Well, it had been out for days before, so they would be okay. They had plenty of candles, oil for the lanterns, bottled water, non-perishable food, and wood for the fireplaces. Sebastian had built a fire in his room last night. Drifting off to sleep, she had smelled the smoke. However, she was starting to miss the taste of milk in her coffee and would appreciate that once power came back on. And right now, she really wanted some good, strong coffee.

She spent a rough night tossing and turning restlessly, waking each time Sebastian shifted on his bed. He sounded rather active, too. She caught herself wondering if he was naturally that way, or if it was just being here, around her, that made him act as such. Or maybe he was cold and kept adding logs to the fire throughout the night. It could be as simple as that.

Of course, if we shared rooms, it would conserve body heat. Gasping, she looked around, guilty at the sudden thought. *Now, where did that naughty little suggestion come from?*

She was through with men, remember? Never again. Never, ever again. She had no reason nor need to conserve body heat with any man, especially one who tapped at her heart with his bewitching green eyes, easy charm, and soulful saxophone.

She lifted the ceramic pitcher and poured water into the basin, and washed off, changing the water to brush her teeth. At least they had plenty of bottled water stored in case the pipes froze. Or she could boil snow to melt for water as well.

Dressed once more for the day's chill, she headed downstairs to see where the handsome and beguiling Sebastian Knight might be.

———

The fall colors drew him in first. Rising, washing at the antique basin in his room, Sebastian stood at the turret windows, analyzing the day. He had to get out and start shooting. And since there was still no power, what better time to take advantage of the cloudy day?

He glanced at the scenery past the rocks leading to the surrounding hills, drawn to the bright foliage of the leaves, dressed in their late-fall colors. Maples, aspens, birch, and oaks dazzled in the early morning sunlight splintering through the clouds in a myriad of yellows and reds, silvers and browns. With enough evergreen pines, spruce, and lots of white snow to add depth, the colors were amazingly breathtaking. His fingers itched to snap the camera lens to capture the scenery.

Almost as much as his fingers itched to stroke the chin of one Raven Koynes and probably get a painful poke from her spines in the process.

"Still no power, huh?" he questioned unnecessarily as he joined her downstairs.

Raven speared him with a dark scowl, and he backed up a step.

"I think I'll go exploring some more after breakfast. Maybe up the hill." He straddled the chair, watching her work. She was so efficient that no movement was a waste. Watching her was like watching productivity personified.

"So there really isn't anyone else here on the island?" he asked. "No one else I could run into?"

"There's plenty you could run into. Moose, bear, cougar, wolf, elk..."

He chuckled. "I was referring more to people. No other people on the island?"

She sent him another wordless glare. "You don't have to wait in here while I am cooking," she pointed out evenly. "You could go in the dining room or the living room. Or out on the porch or gazebo, even. I could call you."

He grinned, tilting his head. "You know, I sometimes get this weird impression you don't want me around, Raven."

She ignored him, focusing instead on the task at hand. She spoke quietly and distinctly. "I was just pointing out it wasn't necessary for you to be around at the meal preparation stages to guarantee you'll be fed."

"You think I'm hanging around, bugging you, just to make sure you feed me?" He started at the suggestion. "Raven, trust me, I am not in here for the food."

Pulling away from the chair, he grabbed his jacket along the way to the front door, where he picked up the camera case he'd left there and headed outside. Yes, she'd call him in time to eat, but he could snap a few pictures near the house until then.

―――――

Blowing out a shaky breath, Raven watched him go, striding off the porch and across the grounds to the dock. His comment, softly assured, made her wonder. There was no mistake she'd insulted him by the way he said it, but how should she take it? Bugging her? Oh yes, the man was bugging her in ways she never knew one could bug. He had a talent for getting under her skin and crawling around in thoughts he had no business creeping through.

Apparently, food was not his motivation for being underfoot. So, what was? That look in his eyes, a certain way he looked at her, when he seemed to be laughing inside, could so easily melt her into a puddle. Right there on the spot, in the kitchen, on the widow's walk, wherever he happened to be when he handed her that incredibly tender and amused look. It bothered her that he could look both tender and amused at the same time. Darn him, it wasn't fair. His expression, so oblivious to him, almost turned her insides out.

And she didn't want him to be looking at her that way. Either way. Not as if he found her amusing, since that was not her intention. And certainly not tenderly. Absolutely not. Those were ways a man looked at a woman he cared about, had feelings for.

She narrowly avoided slicing her thumb with the knife and jerked back, gasping. Oh, the man could upset her. She'd better pay more attention to her culinary chores and less to thoughts of him, or else she'd have no fingers left once he finally departed.

Breakfast preparation finished and table set, she moved to the door to make good on her promise.

———

Behaving like a perfect gentleman, Sebastian savored the meal and the company. He found it remarkable how well she could cook with no power. Simply amazing. And even with her spikes pushed out, warning him, she was still delightful company, albeit rather quiet company. He continued to have the impression she did not like him around, but he was also getting the vibe she didn't really want him to go either, which just added to her mystery.

"So, what are your plans for the day?" he asked as their meal wound down. "Since I pledge to stay outside with my cameras and leave you alone."

She made a *humph* sound. "I don't quite believe I could be rid of you all day. But I'll take what I can get. I have no plans as I never have plans."

"You don't make plans?" She seemed the type to have each detail well-thought-out.

"My days are much the same every day. And I prefer to keep it that way."

He had the suspicion that she would prefer many things. Like the proverbial bumblebee, she was warning him now. He just chose not to heed her warning. "Okay, no more questions, I pledge that too," he promised, hands spread out, though the breaking smirk couldn't be contained. She could be fun to tease if he were careful.

A thumping at the door had his grin fading. Her eyes met his across the table, and he noted the surprise flickering in them.

"Okay, one more question," he said. "Are you expecting more company?"

Shaking her head as she moved, she made it to the door first.

Tall silhouettes on the other side of the lace curtain proved her visitors were human. She was about to open the door when Sebastian noticed that it appeared to swing open before she touched the knob.

A rush of cold air greeted him, along with three people bursting into the room, pushing them both backward with their combined presence.

Two men and one woman, cold pouring off them, swept into the room, stomping snow off their boots.

Snow? Sebastian stared in disbelief. Where had they come from? They each carried backpacks. His gut twisted in warning.

"Well, well, look here," the taller, balding man said, smiling first at Raven and then at Sebastian.

Sebastian could see Raven's disdainful glare at his sneer. Adrenaline coursed through his arteries at the man's suggestive look.

"Who are you?" Raven asked, taking a step back.

Sebastian took a protective step forward, grateful when she silently leaned into him.

"Who we are doesn't matter. It's what we're after," the first man answered.

The woman, a heavy blonde, and the other man, average to the point of being nondescript, prowled the room with their fingers touching everything.

Standing straight, irritation shadowing her delicate features, Raven addressed the balding man. "Please do not manhandle my things. What are you after?"

The man laughed, still wearing a dark sneer. Stepping forward, he reached out, grabbing Raven's arm and twisting, grinning at her sharp intake of breath.

Sebastian lunged, fists curled and a snarl on his breath.

With amazing speed and agility, the nondescript man was upon him, holding him fast.

"Dudley, secure him. Helen, help Dudley," the balding man ordered, retaining the pinching vice grip on Raven's arm despite her thick sweater.

Helpless against two, the people called Helen and Dudley wrestled Sebastian into a Windsor chair and looped ropes around him that the woman pulled from one of their packs. He winced as they tightened the knots.

"Wait!" Raven cried, trying to pull away from the man holding her arm. "We have food and supplies. We will share with you. There is no need for this...extreme."

"Honey, you have not yet seen extreme," the balding man assured, running one finger down Raven's cheek.

Sebastian tugged at the knots, catching her eye, seeing her shudder. "Where did you come from and what do you want with us?" he demanded, barely able to keep the growl from his voice.

"Dudley, you stay here and watch this guy. Helen, come

with me, and we'll take this pretty lady for a walk." Tightening his grip on her arm, the man forced Raven to step forward. Reluctantly, she went, barely biting back the cry of pain.

Sebastian tried to wriggle free. "Only a coward would manhandle a woman like that," he yelled to their retreating backs. "Come back here and act like a man!"

Alone, except for the man referred to as Dudley, Sebastian sat, fuming. *How did I let them get the upper hand and end up bound to the chair? Who are they? Where did they come from with thick snow on their boots? What did they want with Raven?* He wished this Dudley character had gone along, leaving him alone. The actual being tied to a chair was not the problem; the unwanted chaperone was. If he were alone, he'd be free in a matter of seconds. Shifting into any number of animals would work to break free from the ropes. But this way, he'd have to kill Dudley. Or at least shake him up a whole lot.

His gut tightened. What the hell were they doing to Raven?

———

"I don't understand why you feel you have to be so rough," Raven said, stumbling along. "I will cooperate, just let us go. Tell me what you want, and we'll get it for you."

"We're after the treasure, honey," Helen purred.

"What treasure? There's no treasure here."

"Arthur, she said there's no treasure," Helen jeered.

"She's lying," Arthur promised. "Here, inside." He pushed the door to the barn open, shoving her inside, releasing his vice-like grip on her arm.

Stumbling through the moldy straw while kicking up dust, Raven rubbed her sore arm, sure there would be bruises. "Now, what treasure are you talking about?" she demanded, whirling on the pair.

"The treasure that was on board the *Endeavor*. This here island is the only one around where she sank. And you must know where it's at."

"The *Endeavor?*" She racked her brain, trying to recall. *The ship that sank last year off the coast of the island?* Yes, she remembered something about it now. The vessel was supposedly carrying rare coins and artwork for a museum exhibit. Except she got caught in a storm, sank, and her valuable cargo was lost to the lake. There had been recovery attempts, she remembered seeing boats in the area afterward. But to her knowledge, no one had been successful in raising the load or the boat, and the last she knew, the insurance paid it off as a complete loss of both the freight and the *Endeavor*.

"No one raised the cargo or the boat. Both were declared total losses." Her shoulders tensed. She read their faces, hoping they would believe her. Maybe they'd realize this was a wild goose chase and leave.

Arthur laughed. "Ha! That's what everyone was supposed to think. The treasure was salvaged and stored on this island until someone decided the time was deemed safe enough to move. We're here for it now."

Was that possible? She shook her head. Wouldn't she have noticed someone bringing a boatload of freight ashore? Not necessarily. "Well, I certainly know nothing about that or where it could possibly be hiding. I think you are wrong. That treasure is still at the bottom of the lake."

Arthur moved closer, taking her arm again. She almost gagged at his foul breath as he leaned close, putting them nose to nose. "You'll help us find it, or your pal inside is going to pay the price. You got that?"

Can I stall them? Pretend I know something about this?

Until what? I can't handle three of them, and Sebastian certainly isn't able to help me now. And what if this hulking Arthur would really harm Sebastian? Or me, if he thinks I was bluffing? Cold sweat dripped down her spine as she met Arthur's eyes, measuring her few options.

She glanced around the space, looking for...anything. His hot breath fanned her face, and she looked back into his hard gaze. Beside her, Helen shifted, her feet kicking up dust from the straw. Raven's mind went blank. There was nothing she could use to stall or help.

Stalling seemed to be her best defense.

Okay. She drew in a deep breath, pushing her hair behind her. "So, if we find this treasure, how do you plan to get it off the island? I didn't see a boat at the dock."

Helen drew her lips into a pout. "We got blown off course in the storm and crashed our boat on the other side of this island," she explained. "We hiked through the woods to get here. We can take your boat to leave."

Her eyebrows shot upward. "You hiked?" The interior of the island was rugged and treacherous in the wintertime. A thought occurred to her. "You must be hungry and tired. Come back inside the house and untie my friend. We can provide you with food and a warm place to rest and wash up. Then we can discuss the cargo on the *Endeavor*."

She thought Helen might go for her tempting suggestion. The woman's eyes darted around, running it over in her mind.

"Enough," Arthur barked. "Helen, back inside. Watch the boyfriend and send Dudley out here. We're sticking with the plan."

"Yes, Arthur, the plan." Contrite, Helen shuffled to the barn door, head down, and kicking up dust in her wake.

"As for you," Arthur whirled, grabbing Raven's arm, "you and I are going to talk about this cargo right now."

Fidgeting under the ropes, Sebastian wondered if it would do any good to try talking to Dudley. The guy didn't seem too terribly bright. Maybe he could convince him to loosen the ropes, and he'd not have to shift. Or at least to leave the room so he could. Either option was acceptable. The sooner, the better, he could find Raven and that bald thug. Studying his guard, contemplating his words, he heard the front door open.

Were they coming back with Raven? He perked up, head swiveling to the doorway. She had better be unharmed. Or else they may all see something shocking.

Helen entered. Alone. She slowly sauntered to Dudley. "Arthur wants you in the barn. To help. I can watch him." She nodded toward Sebastian.

Needles pricked along the back of his neck. There was something about her that worried him. More so than Dudley did. Obedient, Dudley shuffled out the door without a word. Helen watched him go, then swept around the room again.

"Cozy," she said, slowly dragging her fingertips over picture frames and figurines. "Fancy, even." Coming behind Sebastian, she rested her fire engine red fingertips on his shoulder, lightly drumming.

He tensed, and dread settled in his stomach. Each tap-tap-tap of those red nails sent cold shivers along his arms and down his spine.

"You know, handsome, Dudley and my brother are going to get what they want from her. When Arthur is on a mission, there is no stopping him." She trailed her fingers along his neck, raising hairs in her wake, along to his jaw. "However, if you were to cooperate, I can make it easy on you."

She stroked her fingers along his jaw, sliding around in front of him, hand cupping his chin. "I like you. I can make it so my brother doesn't hurt you."

"What about Raven?" They better not have touched her. He fought to keep the growl out of his voice.

Helen shrugged. "Yeah, her too, probably. Depends on whether she cooperates. It's you I'm thinking about here. You have such pretty eyes."

Sebastian grimaced as she ran a hand slowly through his hair, sure he was going to be sick. But now he knew what game she was playing.

"Well, I can't really do anything, tied up like I am." He mustered up a smile, hoping it looked genuine.

Helen smiled back, cupping his chin once more, her other hand moving south. "Oh yes, you can, honey." Grabbing a handful of hair, she threw one leg over his, her mouth moving for his lips.

"Hey! Uh, there's a knife in the kitchen," he sputtered quickly. "Go get it and cut me loose. It'll be easier for me that way." He wore his best willing smile as he swallowed the churning bile at the back of his throat. To his relief, she lifted herself off and struck out for the kitchen. Not waiting for her to disappear into the other room, he had already selected his method of escape.

He concentrated as the bracelet on his wrist sizzled. Fur pushed through his skin. Whiskers extended alongside his nose. His teeth lengthened. The bonds fell away, and he lithely bound for the door.

CHAPTER
FOUR

"Okay, fine, girlie," Arthur said. "I think you believe there's no treasure. A person can convince themselves of anything. But I also think you'll change your mind soon enough."

Raven swallowed hard. She had to remain calm to get out of this alive. Her gaze flicked from Arthur to Dudley and back to Arthur. He obviously was the more volatile of the two men. And his height, ample girth, and sullen features added to the intimidation.

She swung her gaze around the barn, wishing answers to her predicament were scrawled on the aged wood. Unfortunately, they were not. She'd have to think of something to pacify them for now. She took one step away from Arthur, raising more dust in her wake. He followed with another step toward her, as if worried she would go bursting from the barn and run away to freedom.

They were on an isolated island. In the wake of the nor'easter storm. Where was she supposed to run off to?

She sidestepped Arthur's grip, almost gagging on his foul odor. *Halitosis? BO? Whatever it is, it is terrible.*

"The treasure hardly matters. Even if you had the cargo,

you would still be as stranded here just as we are. If you have cell phones, you have no reception here. And until the power comes on, there is no phone to call anyone. I have no Internet or boat. Plus, if you did call someone, you'd have to wait for them to arrive."

"She's got some good points, Arthur," Dudley murmured through a lisp. He immediately looked down at the straw, as if afraid to match the larger man's eye.

"Yeah, yeah," Arthur said. "We hadn't planned on losing the boat. And since Dudley here says there's no other boats around, which I don't totally believe myself yet, we'll meet you halfway. For now." His steely gaze made Raven's stomach clench. His hot breath blowing into her face made her want to heave.

Onions and garlic? Raw fish? God, whatever it is, I'm going to wretch.

"Great," she said coolly, fighting for composure. "So we'll go back to the house, you'll release my friend, and we'll go from there? I imagine your sister would appreciate a place to clean up and rest?"

"Fine," Arthur agreed, just as coolly.

Heart pounding, Raven headed for the door and relative freedom. At least freedom for Sebastian until they could think of something else. Would he even know about the *Endeavor* and her priceless cargo? How far had the stories spread in the papers?

"Hey, Arthur," Dudley cried. "I thought I just saw a cougar out here."

"Is it still around?"

"No."

"Then who cares? It probably ran back to the woods."

———

55

Sebastian barely had time to reach the house, work his claws to open the door, and slip inside. Hearing Helen in the kitchen, he raced for the living room, feeling his teeth and whiskers retracting as he went. By the time he reached the chair, he had hands again. He scooped up his clothes, hastily pulling them on.

As he was tying his boots, Helen came from one direction and the other three from the opposite direction.

"Hey, what are you doing loose already?" Arthur snarled, turning to Helen, where she stood holding a knife.

"I'm an escape artist in my spare time," Sebastian said, plastering a grin onto his face. "I always wanted to be Houdini as a kid. So, what's going on?"

He tried to act neutral, but it was hard.

Glancing at her, he could see obvious relief in her eyes. Relief he was safe and free? His chest loosened. And he mentally made a solemn vow that he would do what he needed to keep her safe. He blinked in surprise as she took two small steps near him, stopped herself, and gripped the nearest chairback. Her dark eyes locked onto him, and her lips parted, and he had to wonder; had she wanted to come to his side?

If so, what stopped her? He'd have welcomed her and hoped to ease the strain around her eyes. He watched her draw in three deep breaths, subtle, but he noticed them. His gaze flicked to the others, and they all appeared oblivious. She collected herself, slowly exhaling. Perhaps she felt it better not to encourage these jerks to create their thoughts on his and Raven's relationship.

Was it only yesterday he landed on her island and hoped she wouldn't send him packing? And now he was ready to protect her in any way...or form.

"So, what's all this about?" He kept his voice calm.

"A boat sank off the west shore last year. Part of her

cargo was paintings, art, and gold coins." Raven waved her hand collectively at the three visitors. "They are after the riches of the *Endeavor*. She went down around April."

"Hmm," Sebastian said, racking his brain for words to diffuse the tense situation. "Last April I was in the Congo, shooting gorillas and waterfalls." At Arthur's surprised glance, he added, "I'm a nature photographer by trade."

"You know, Arthur, as big as this place is, it could be stashed somewhere inside," Dudley pointed out, eyeing the vaulted ceilings and endless cubbyholes.

"Yeah, yeah, I already figured that out. Before we are done, little Miss Hospitality here will have shown us every nook and cranny of the house and every building on this island. Seems like we have nothing but time." Folding into a chair, leaning back, Arthur ran his gaze over Raven, grinning hungrily.

Sebastian barely resisted the urge to rush forward, plowing one into his smug jowls. He couldn't afford to get tied to a chair again with a full audience. From the corner of his eye, he caught Raven's scarcely suppressed shudder as she turned from Arthur. Her lips pressed tight, and her face paled. Sebastian's blood heated. Asshole had better stay away from her.

"Now," Arthur said, "I believe you said something about food?"

Watching Raven, Sebastian knew she was a master of grace under pressure. He had to admire her for that. But watching their intruders, slivers of anxiety gnawed at him. Arthur was entirely too interested in Raven, eyeballing her like a besotted hound. And Helen could barely keep her hands off *him*. She behaved like a randy deer. He suspected it was mostly her brother's presence that kept her in line. What a predicament.

All he wanted to do was take Raven into his arms, hold

her close, and keep her safe. But he forced himself to keep a casual distance. And follow Raven's lead to keep physical distance and eye contact to a minimum.

He needed a way to get close to her without anyone suspecting a thing. Watching Raven now, he thought he had the perfect plan.

———

Raven bristled, teeth clenched, as she prepared three plates and set them around the table. She cast a brief glance at Sebastian where he stood across the room and swallowed back a groan. Now that she wanted him underfoot, Sebastian seemed to keep a safe distance.

He finally picks now to give me my space? Seriously?

She set the Dutch oven with the warmed beef stew in the center of the table and dropped a ladle into it, watching it settle in the thick broth.

While Sebastian wasn't completely out of her eyesight, he still wasn't close enough to offer a reassuring touch she so badly needed right now. Raven wasn't sure which upset her more, Sebastian not rushing to her rescue or these...thugs for crashing into her home and holding them both hostage. Well, they were likely stranded here for several more days, so they had to all work out some sort of mutual coexistence. Maybe in time, she could show them she knew nothing about the *Endeavor's* lost cargo.

She could only hope the power came on soon and these three would leave. But then would she be alone with Sebastian once more, or would he leave too?

———

An hour later, Raven made her way down to the shore. She considered this horrible mess while standing on the rocks, staring at the water. Tears brimming in her eyes, she fought them by biting her bottom lip. Arthur and company were busy rummaging around her house, looking for that darn treasure. Searching the house, going through her possessions, it felt like they were personally violating her, just without the physical touch.

Unable to watch them yank open drawers, rifle through shelves, and paw through everything else, she informed them she was going outside for some fresh air, and they would just have to deal with that.

She was surprised they allowed her to go, but she was even more startled when Sebastian didn't offer to tag along. Since when? Now that she wanted him near her so badly, she could imagine him drawing her into a protective embrace. Her skin heated as the thought took root. *Why isn't he protecting me?*

She curled her fists into balls, clenched tight in her pockets, as she stared at the horizon where the water met the sky. Nothing. There was absolutely nothing out there. In all the years she had lived here on the island, this was the first time she felt alone. Darn, the tears were going to come after all.

A soft whine caught her attention. Looking around, she spotted a dog making its way along the rocks toward her. Black in color, with brown spots, and it was a big dog. A *really* big, powerful-looking dog. Maybe a German Shepherd? She liked dogs but didn't know what the breeds were called. She knelt and offered her hand.

"Here, doggie," she called softly. "Where did you come from?"

The dog reached her side and stood there, wagging its tail, looking at her with hope.

"Sorry, big fella, I don't have any dog treats," she offered. "Did you fall out of some passing boat during the storm?" Reaching out to touch the silky fur, she frowned. "You're not wet, or even damp. If you came ashore in the storm, you dried off quickly." Her fingers worked through its neck, exploring. "Do you have a collar or ID of any kind?"

The dog instantly pulled away before she could reach through the thick fur on his neck.

"Okay, fine, I won't check for ID, just don't leave me right now, okay?" She hated the misery in her voice, even for a dog to hear, but his quiet presence made her suddenly feel better. How could she keep the dog with her?

"Stay?" she whispered, upset at her vulnerability. The dog returned to her side and looked up at her with dark, adoring eyes. His tongue lolled out, revealing large, white, razor-sharp teeth.

"Hey, fella, I might have a soup bone inside you can chew on. Sorry, but it's the best I can do." She petted him between his ears. "You are a pretty thing. Since I can't tell if you have ID or a name already, I need to call you something while you're here." She paused, turning her head to one side, grinning slightly. "I hate to tell you this, fella, but you're just as stranded as the rest of them right now. Even a dog can't swim to the mainland."

Aware she was rambling to a dog, it nonetheless felt good. The dog sat at her feet, leaning against her. It was as if he were giving her a canine hug. As her hand stilled, he gave her a tender lick with his tongue.

"I don't mind this, fella, in fact, I kind of like it. But there are these bad people inside my house right now. And I hope you're not this nice to them. In fact, if you bite one of them, I'd be okay with that. You seem so friendly now, but you look like you could be intimidating if you wanted to be. And I hope you will be once you see those terrible people."

Lying down, the dog rested one paw on her foot, gazing into her eyes. If a dog could offer understanding and comfort, she felt she was witnessing it right here. She was probably crazy to even think he could understand her, but immediately she loved the large dog.

"I don't know where you came from, but I sure am glad you're here. Do you mind if I call you Salzburg?"

Salzburg, the Shepherd, seemed content to follow her around the rest of the afternoon. She wandered the shore, studied the autumn colors on the trees, and ended up at the gazebo. Her new pal never left her side. And Sebastian never appeared. Maybe they had him inside with them, tied to a chair again. Unable to know if it was true, and not able to help him if he were, she decided to stay outside longer. It would take them a while to rampage her house, and even longer for her to fix the mess she assumed they would leave in their wake.

Darn the *Endeavor* and her stupid cargo and the storm that took her down. Damn these degenerates for invading her life like they were doing. What happened to her quiet little life? Peaceful and all the solitude she could wish for. Fresh tears brimmed in her eyes, burning with hot saltiness.

Salzburg roused from her feet, jumped up, placing both front feet on her lap, and sticking his nose even with hers, whining softly.

"Oh, I'm okay, just feeling sorry for myself," she said, hugging the dog and laying her head against his furry shoulder. "And here I am crying about me, and I don't even know what happened to Sebastian. I can only hope he's okay. I don't like him much, but I'd hate to think they're harming him."

Salzburg licked her cheek, slapping a paw against her leg.

"I'm so glad you're here with me now, Salzburg," she murmured, burying her nose in his fur. She drew back, sniffing carefully. "For a dog who I think took a long swim in the cold lake recently, you sure smell fresh and clean. And you're in good shape, so I know whatever happened to you must've happened recently. I sure wish you could talk to me."

————

"What's that?" Arthur demanded as Raven and Salzburg entered the house. He pointed a crooked finger at her and Salzburg, stopping them at the threshold between the parlor and dining room.

"This is my dog, and you better be nice to him." She rested her hand on his head, level with her thigh, and breathed a sigh of relief as the dog lifted his lips to Arthur, showing a hint of white teeth and growling softly, low in his deep chest. She could have dropped to the floor and hugged him again.

"Keep that mutt away from me," Arthur warned.

"This dog goes where he wants to go," Raven countered, her eyes sweeping the room. No sign of Sebastian. The chair he had been bound to before was empty, with the ropes where he had maneuvered out of them. The house, as she figured, was trashed. Huffing, she glared at Arthur, hands on her hips.

"Did you have to make such a mess? Maybe now you can believe your stupid treasure isn't here. And what have you done with Sebastian?"

"I haven't done anything with him. Last I saw him, he and Helen were headed outside. Together." Arthur took a step toward her, raising a hand. "And mark my words, that treasure is here."

Raven watched as Salzburg flattened his ears, showing all his teeth, his growl deep and throaty. Barking once, he advanced, meeting Arthur's step.

Arthur stepped back, lowering his hand. "Keep that mutt away from me," he warned. "Or else you'll be missing a dog as well as a boyfriend."

Arthur's face paled, and a gasp escaped him. He whirled, swiftly striding from the room. Within a minute, the back door slammed. A peaceful silence followed his speedy exit.

Raven swept Salzburg into her arms. "Oh, thank you, dog! A hundred thank yous. I can't tell you how much he creeps me out, and to know he is scared of you, well, that's more priceless to me than all the *Endeavor's* supposed treasure. Come on, let's find you a soup bone." Maybe she'd thaw a package of moose ribs for him too.

———

By dinnertime, Raven had some of the house restored to an acceptable state, with much more to do. And her dog was gone. She concluded someone must've let him outside. He'd never asked to go out. He'd spent a few hours lying in whatever room she was cleaning, and suddenly, she went to the kitchen and noticed he was gone.

She could only hope he came back. Turning the steaming pot on the stove down to simmer, figuring if anyone was hungry, they could help themselves, she startled as Sebastian walked into the room.

"Hi," he greeted her. "How are you?"

"Where have you been?" Scanning the room, assuring herself they were alone, she rushed into his arms. Quickly, she buried her nose in his shoulder before the tears could fall again.

"Hey," he whispered, hugging her close and stroking her hair. "Are you okay?"

"No. I'm not okay. How could I be?"

"It's going to be all right, Raven, honestly, it will." He paused a moment before his hand resumed the rhythmic caress. She closed her eyes at the pleasure of his touch and his rumbling voice soft at her ear. "I honestly wasn't expecting this sort of reception from you, but I'm here now, and it's all going to be fine."

Drawing back, she slammed her fists into his chest. She knew she had caught him off guard by the startled gasp and shock in his eyes. Enraged, she yelled, "How dare you. Darn you, Sebastian Knight. Where have you been all day?"

Chuckling, he caught her hands. "Now there are the sharp pokes I'm used to seeing with you." Drawing her back to him, he inhaled deeply. "You're so wild and windy, Raven. I want to kiss you right now, hard and fast."

She drew back, tears stinging her eyes. *He did? So why doesn't he?*

"Raven, oh, Raven. You've been so brave, don't lose it now. Don't let them think for a second they might be getting to you."

She stared at his mouth. He wanted to kiss her, hard and fast. Her mouth watered. *How would he taste? As good as he smelled?*

Impetuously, she reached up to meet him, grabbing his lower lip in her teeth, demanding the promised kiss. As he pulled her close once more, she closed her eyes, stretching to wrap both arms around his neck, keeping him close. He tasted clean and fresh, and if she didn't know better, she'd swear he'd had beef stew lately. His hands curled around her hair, weaving it through his fingers, then he cupped the back of her head and pressed it close to his face.

He moaned. She pulled back as heat spread between them. Keeping her eyes locked with his, she licked her lips. Her anger dimmed, for the moment. "Why did you go away? When I needed you here with me." She hated that she sounded wimpy and quickly brushed the tears falling on her cheeks.

He pushed her back at arm's length, cupping her jaw in his palms. "When they said they were searching the house, you looked so broken. I couldn't take it. I had to get away for a while. I hated to leave you alone. It was selfish of me. I'm sorry."

"Arthur said he saw you and Helen leave together."

He grimaced and rolled his eyes. "I ditched her as soon as I rounded the corner of the house. She's probably still out there looking for me."

"I wasn't alone. A dog came to me. Down by the water." Lowering her voice, she whispered near his ear, "He just came out of nowhere, over the rocks along the shore, but he acts like I'm his long-lost owner. I've never seen him before. But Arthur is really scared of him. Salzburg is so big, powerful, and fierce-looking."

"Wow. That's great. Salzburg, huh? That's a strong German name. Is he a German Shepherd dog?"

She blushed. "Maybe. I think so. Honestly, I don't know my breeds very well, but I do love dogs."

Sebastian smiled softly. "That's okay. There are several big German breeds that are great protectors. Rottweilers also come to mind. Either would be effective for keeping that Arthur creep away. So where is this monster dog now?" He looked around, as if he might spot the animal lying under a table somewhere.

"I guess someone let him out, and he's gone now." She

blinked rapidly, sniffling, "I hope he comes back again. I gave him a soup bone."

Chuckling heartily, Sebastian pulled her back into his arms. "In that case, I'm sure he will be back. Most likely, he just went to get himself something to eat. If he knows how much you need him, he'll come back to you."

Hoping and wishing so, Raven leaned into his arms, closing her eyes and breathing deeply. For now, Sebastian was here, and they were both safe. Heaven only knows what the evening would bring.

———

"There are five bedrooms in this house," Raven announced once Arthur and his company assembled in the living room.

Sebastian added more wood to the fire and waited for the crackling to stop before speaking. "The chairs down here are quite comfortable."

Raven laid a hand on his arm, wishing he would shut up. "Since we still have no power, each bedroom has a fireplace and enough water jugs to fulfill your needs. There are ample candles and oil lanterns and lots of blankets as well."

"We could double up, sharing beds to share heat," Helen suggested, her eyes bright on Sebastian.

Raven bit back a cringe, aware of Arthur's steady gaze trained on Sebastian.

"My sister has taken a fancy to you, pretty boy," Arthur observed before looking over at Raven. "However, she has a good idea about doubling up." He reached up to scratch his chin.

"There is plenty of heat from the fireplaces and blankets," Raven asserted. "I seriously think doubling up will not be necessary. Unless it was purely for personal gratification," she added with disgust, eyeing Helen.

Helen delivered a tart smile, a dark gap in place of where her front tooth had been. At the window, she peeled back the curtain, and the light of the full moon flooded the room. "I have a better idea," she said, going to her brother and whispering in his ear.

Arthur looked shocked.

Raven strained to hear their conversation with dread rolling around in her stomach. She cast a glance at Sebastian, knowing this was going to be bad. First, a chill rolled over her, then a new thought hit her. *They wouldn't?*

Her stomach rolled as hot nausea rushed up her throat. She pressed a hand to her mouth, and her cheeks puffed, as she willed herself not to vomit.

"Are you sure?" Arthur asked Helen. "It's cold."

She nodded quickly, pink coloring her cheeks.

Resigned, Arthur motioned for Dudley and whispered in his ear as Helen disappeared up the winding steps.

Catching Raven's puzzled glance, Sebastian shrugged, just as Dudley and Arthur rushed him, pulling his arms behind his back.

"Hey," he yelled as his body wriggled in protest.

"What are you doing?" Raven demanded hotly, surging forward.

Arthur shoved her away, angering Sebastian. Letting out a growl of fury, he was stunned as Arthur cuffed him soundly behind the ear.

Raven reeled back at his action. Sputtering, she demanded, "Stop," and followed them outside.

Ignoring her protests, Dudley and Arthur dragged Sebastian, cursing and twisting, to the boathouse and bodily forced him down by a stout pole.

"Wait! Stop this insanity," Raven shouted. She tried to block Dudley, using herself as a shield.

Arthur wordlessly grabbed her arm and handed her off to Dudley. She never felt so powerless, like a child.

"My sister has a better idea," Arthur stated simply, twisting lengths of rope Dudley supplied around Sebastian. "Now let's see you get out of these knots, Houdini. She'll be along shortly." He gave a chuckle. "To share body heat."

"You have no right—" Raven argued until Arthur grabbed her arm, wrenching it backward, painfully twisting her skin. She bit back a cry.

"If you don't settle down, you'll get the same as him. As it is, consider yourself lucky I'm not so inclined. Not just yet anyway."

Arthur's warning snarl stilled her. He leaned so close; she could count the wrinkles on his face. His hot, vile breath slammed her senses like an exploding balloon. She blinked. His vice-like hold kept her from taking a step back.

His threat, which she believed he'd carry out, combined with his halitosis, gagged her. She coughed and pressed her free hand to her mouth.

Repulsed by his sour breath and leering glance, she cast a hopeless look at Sebastian. What could she do to help him when she feared what tonight would bring her?

His calmness surprised her. She swore he gave her a quick wink, but she must've been wrong. She also thought he wore a confident grin, but she must be reading him wrong.

He shook his head at her. "Go on," he urged. "I'll be fine."

———

As it was, Sebastian barely resisted shifting, rushing forward, and snapping Arthur's neck. Those three degenerates had better get off the island soon, or he was going to do something to land himself in jail.

Sebastian was sure Raven tasted blood from how hard she bit her lip. Raven nodded to him, blinked rapidly, and whirled.

Arthur and Dudley moved to the door, closing it behind them, dropping the heavy bar into place.

Sebastian could hear them laughing as they walked away, assuming he was held fast until Helen arrived.

No way. Closing his eyes, the bracelet grew warm, sizzling. He felt feathers poking through his skin, his ears pulling back into his head. Within seconds, he was free and flying up through the open window. Not seeing any sign of Helen yet, he landed and shaped back into his human form. Lifting the bar on the door, he went in and gathered his clothes. Dressed, leaving the ropes looped around the pole and knots tight, he exited the building, pausing long enough to drop the bar back in place. She would never figure this one out.

Minutes later, he stood on Raven's bedroom balcony. He flew up and changed back to test that she had not locked the door to her bedroom. Having a private way in, he closed his eyes, concentrating again. Soon, the change occurred.

———

Raven lay huddled in bed, fists curled to her chest. Anger burned inside her, warring with sheer helplessness and fear, emotions she could not recall the last time she felt. Until recently.

Loneliness poked in there as well, making for a cocktail of misery. Chewing her lip, she refused to give in to the tears. She was not going to cry.

A soft whine snapped her from her thoughts, and she swung her head to the balcony door.

"Salzburg," she cried. The weight of the dog crawling onto her bed chased away the loneliness and fear. "You're back. But how did you get here? How did you get up onto the balcony? Oh, it doesn't matter, I'm just so glad you're back." Pulling him into a hug, she buried her nose into his shoulder, sobs shaking her.

"You won't believe what happened. Oh, poor Sebastian. I feel so bad for him. He looked so brave a little while ago. I hate Helen, I hate her. I hate her worse than I do Arthur right now."

Salzburg lay next to her, his big body between her and the hallway door, a paw on her lap as she talked nonstop to him.

"Remember earlier when I said I didn't really like Sebastian much? Well, that was kind of a fib. I guess I kind of like him after all. And not just because of tonight. But even before. It started when I caught him playing the saxophone. I never knew one could have that effect on me. But he looked so...I don't know, something. It just tugged at my heart, and I crumbled. I can't really explain it, but do you know what I mean?"

Salzburg whined once, gently pawing her. Encouraged, she continued. "You see, I can't tell him why I'm here, but it's because of another man. One I was married to. It ended horribly, and I came here." She stopped, drawing a deep breath. "Well, when I came here, I said I'd never get involved with a man again. Never risk that sort of hurt again. But when I watched him in the gazebo, playing that saxophone and scribbling in that notebook, I forgot all that past stuff. It was like it never happened."

She laughed once, ending with a sobbing hiccup. "It was one of those perfect romantic nights too. Like in the movies. The moon was almost full, and twilight was falling. He was so handsome in the lantern glow. I wanted to go kiss him. I wanted him to kiss me back. Just like we did earlier tonight in the living room. Oh, you can't imagine how good he made me feel in those few moments. Shameless, isn't it, Salzburg? I wanted so much more than a kiss. I still do."

The dog whined, rolling over and rubbing a paw over his muzzle.

"Oh, come on." Raven laughed at his antics. "It wasn't so bad. At least I had the grace to go back inside before he noticed me. The night on the gazebo, I mean. And the kiss, well, it was worth waiting for. I was probably drooling over myself by then. You know what was really shameless? Not so long ago, I had a naughty thought of sharing a bed with him too. Not the crazy stuff Helen is probably doing now, but just to share equally." She gave a little laugh as her cheeks warmed, glad she was alone in the dark with only a dog. "It was a passing, naughty thought. But he can't ever know I thought any of that stuff about him, okay?"

Salzburg reached up, licking her face once, his brown eyes steady on her face.

"You know, it's crazy, but sometimes I look at him, like tonight, and want him to just kiss me, long and hard. I can imagine us alone, and goosebumps cover my body. I want him to lie with me on the sofa or the bed. And other times, he can upset me so that I'd like to slap him."

Salzburg locked his brown-eyed gaze on her, whined softly, and offered her hand a gentle lick. She looked at her hand.

"That was such a warm, dry lick. I always thought dogs gave wet, slobbery kisses. Like you'd need a towel afterward. That wasn't so different from a kiss by a man." She paused to fan herself with her hand and expelled a long breath. "I wonder how Sebastian's chaste kiss would feel? Or a French kiss? Or a deep, passionate, and heated kiss?"

The Shepherd whined again, his gaze still on her face. She threw her other hand over her forehead as she looked at the dog. She knew dogs could be smart, but this one was almost eerie in how he seemed to understand her. His soulful expression was both tender and comically serious. "I know, don't look at me that way, okay? I know I'm all over the map with him. But you have to remember where I'm coming from. When I first came here, I was twisted up inside with hurt and confusion.

"I guess I stayed that way all this time. But Sebastian has reached into my heart and started unraveling that painful mess. But you have to know, it's not easy for me to let go. Trust again. Hoping again. But when he gives me that look, that special look of his, it about makes me do all those things. Do you think he even has a clue what he can do to me when he looks at me like that? Do you think I'm hopeless, Salzburg?"

The dog offered her another lick, followed by a paw slap and whine.

"I just feel so bad for him out there with that horrible Helen right now. I wish there was something I could do to stop it. Break it up and maybe rescue him. But I don't know what I could do. And to be honest, I would be afraid of Arthur's retaliation."

She pulled the dog into another hug, burying her nose into his thick fur. "You smell musky, but I am glad you are here with me. For the first time in years, I have someone I can talk to. Someone who listens to what I am saying. And with you being a dog, I know my secrets are safe with you, right?"

CHAPTER
FIVE

Raven awoke to early rays of sunlight streaming through the windows, flooding the room. Her fingers threaded through a warm, furry mass. Looking down, Salzburg gazed at her, waiting.

"You weren't a dream after all," she said softly, ruffling his ears.

She shivered, remembering Arthur's anger during the dark hours of the night. He'd come to her room, rattling the knob. Thankfully, she'd taken to locking it with those characters in the house. Finding the door shut and the lock not turning, he roared, slamming his fists against the wood. She was sure the old door would give under his fisted rage.

Salzburg advanced on the door, barking and growling. She could see his white teeth shining in the dark room. He emanated a protective energy. Even if the door gave way, Arthur would only get to her by going through Salzburg first. And he sounded as enraged as Arthur.

Stroking the dog, she realized how precarious her position was right now. Sebastian could barely protect himself; Dudley was of no use, and she was dependent on Salzburg.

"I need to give you some real meat today. How does a moose's liver sound?"

Stretching, she climbed out of bed and stepped to the wash basin. "Good thing you're just a dog," she said, pulling her nightshirt over her head. She tossed it on the bed, next to him, and poured out the water. "Wish I could take an actual bath, but I'll be quick," she promised, starting her bird bath. "Once the power returns, I am taking a long soak in the tub and a real shower, extra hot."

Salzburg looked at the closed door, resting his head on his paws until she was finished. Once she was dressed, he woofed once.

"What's wrong? I thought you wanted moose liver. Do you have to go out?"

At the last word, he perked up, yipping again, wagging his tail.

"Okay, I get it. Let's go." She opened the front door, moving aside as Salzburg brushed by her. "Be careful," she called softly to him. "And, please, come back."

With a bark, he disappeared around the corner of the house.

Turning back, her gaze fell on the boathouse. *Should I go down there? What if Helen is down there?* She couldn't bear that. Deciding Sebastian seemed able to take care of himself, she shut the door, leaving it cracked in case Salzburg returned.

In the meantime, she had a house to clean up, meals to prepare, and to mentally prepare herself for another day with her uninvited guests.

She put moose liver in the sink to thaw, built up the fire, laid out the contents for omelets, and put coffee on the stove to percolate. Then she went upstairs to her room to wait for everyone to arrive.

She heard the door slam while coming back downstairs

when she heard Arthur's loud voice booming like a gunshot.

"Did you rest well, pretty boy?"

"Fair enough," Sebastian answered coolly.

Raven crept to the bottom steps, kneeling to listen to their conversation.

"My sister is disappointed."

"Tough, I'm not her boy toy. And I suggest you never do anything like that again." Sebastian's voice was hard, steady.

Arthur tried to laugh. "And what if I do?"

"In some places, in some cultures, trying a stunt like that could get a person killed," he explained slowly, distinctly. "You might not be so lucky next time. Or her."

Raven could hear Arthur coming out of a chair. Oh no, they were going to go at it. Gripping the stair railings, she peered around the corner.

"Are you threatening me?" Arthur demanded, shoving his shoulder into Sebastian.

"No, I'm promising you." Thrusting his own shoulder into Arthur's, he moved past. "Now, excuse me, but I am going upstairs to my room to change clothes."

Stairs? He's heading for me! Darting back up the steps, she whirled in time to meet him as he reached the top.

"Are you alright?" she asked, hating that she sounded a little breathless.

"I'll feel better once I brush my teeth and clean up. I'd love a real shower."

"Sorry, no power yet." She ached to return to his arms. What if he knew what she had confessed to the dog during the night? Heat warmed through her at the thought.

"Oh well, you did warn me it took a while to come back. So, where's your pooch?" He looked around, as though the dog might be standing behind her.

She shook her head. "He wanted to run this morning. Just a little while ago." Her voice dropped. "I think his being here all night is what kept Arthur away." She described the abridged version of Arthur's visitation attempt.

"In that case, we'd better hope he comes back again."

"It's funny that he doesn't smell like the lake does. He smells fresh and clean, with a little musk. Shouldn't he still smell like the lake if that's where he swam in from?" She mused, tapping the rail with her fingertips.

He captured her fingers, kissing them briefly. "I was just thinking of the railing of the widow's walk where we talked and of Helen's fingers drumming along my body. Trust me when I say there is no comparison whose fingers I want crawling on me."

She warmed at his indication. And his touch. And lips. "Helen is..." Words failed her.

"Like a lioness in season."

She smiled at the comparison. Why did that terrible woman have to be on her island?

"Maybe he swam in before the storm came and has been living in the woods and hills long enough for the smell to wear off?"

"Maybe," she said slowly. "Either way, I hope he comes back." What if he didn't, and she had no protection from Arthur? What if she had no one to talk to again? Talking nonstop to the dog last night was cleansing. Silly perhaps, but wholly cleansing, nonetheless. Apart from the comfort of his protection, the big dog also gave her company. Lifting her eyes to Sebastian, who also seemed lost in his own thoughts, she had to wonder...

No, she wasn't going to do it. Pushing the naughty thought aside again, she straightened up, clearing her throat.

"I did not mean to hold you up." Moving past him, she caught his bewildered look as she started down the steps.

———

"No, absolutely not, I will not," Raven stated half an hour later, arms folded across her chest. "You want the darn cargo, you go find it by yourself." Glaring at Arthur, she huffed indignantly.

Wishing Salzburg was nearby, she nonetheless stuck to her guns. Truly, she had nothing to lose.

Sebastian came down the stairs, carrying another camera case. His eyebrows rose as he looked at Arthur, then at Raven.

"What's going on now?" he asked, setting the case down on the side table by the stairs.

Raven huffed again, flinging her hand at Arthur and Helen. "He, *they*, want me to go treasure hunting for them. Like they actually think I know, or even care, where that darn stuff is. If it even is here, which I doubt. And I still have this house to straighten up from their shakedown yesterday. Are they offering to help fix their damage? No! So why should I help them in some stupid, silly, wild goose chase? No, I will not do it!"

Sebastian crossed the floor to stand near her, folded his arms, and regarded Arthur. The balding man was not happy. Whether it was her refusal to help or Sebastian's supportive presence, Raven did not know, nor did she care.

"Well, that about sums it up, I guess. Why do you find it so hard to believe she isn't aware of anything about this cargo? If she doesn't know, she doesn't know."

Arthur shook a finger at Raven, scowling. "She lived here when the boat sank. She has to know what happened.

She's lying to keep it for herself. We're not leaving without it."

Raven threw her hands in the air, exasperation making her breathless. "I never saw anything except some recovery boats the day after the *Endeavor* sank. No one, at any time, came to the island. And I certainly would not keep some dumb coins and artwork for myself. And you most certainly are leaving, as soon as it can be arranged when the power returns."

Sebastian smiled.

Whirling, Raven picked up some throw pillows that had been recklessly tossed aside yesterday. "I have a house to tidy. If you want food, go get it yourself," she spat over her shoulder. "Same for that darn treasure. I am tired of this nonsense," she complained, carefully placing the pillows where they originally were. "Darn you all. I want you gone, all of you gone!"

Tears blinded her eyes as she straightened a couple of photos. Behind her, boots clomped and shuffled as they headed outside. "Good luck to the lot of you. Maybe you'll get lost and never return. Or get eaten by a bear. I don't care," she yelled as the door closed.

Someone touched her shoulder, and she jumped, whirling, hand flying to her chest.

"Sorry, I didn't mean to startle you," Sebastian spoke, his voice rumbling softly by her ear.

"I thought I was alone."

"Raven, I have one thing I need to do, then I'll be back and help you finish straightening up this mess, okay?"

"That would be nice." His lopsided smile made her wonder what he was up to.

"Good, save some work for me. I'll be back soon." His smile broadened, and her heart skipped a couple of beats as he took her into his arms. He lowered his mouth and kissed her, long and deep like she had wistfully spoken of last night. Her fingers crawled up his neck, and the heat within him simmered like a boiling pot. As it heated within her.

Exhaling a low breath, he held her by the shoulders. His gentle touch, protective and altogether suggestive, matched the heavy look in his eyes. She licked her lips. Mint from his toothpaste landed on her taste buds.

"You looked like you needed that," he said softly, releasing her completely.

Reeling, Raven dropped onto the nearest chair. He was gone, leaving his cameras inside, leaving her breathless.

―――――

Standing at the shoreline, balanced on two rocks, Sebastian stuffed his hands in his pockets. After that kiss with Raven, he needed to cool down a bit. When she smiled at him, licking her lips in the most seductive way, he'd bet she didn't even know what she was doing. But if she kept it up, he was going to have to kiss her like that again. Excitement pulsed through him at the idea, and images of the future followed.

Pulling her into his arms, he cradled her head and gave in to kiss those oh-so-kissable lips. It was delightful when her softness pressed into him. As her arms went around his waist, fingers connected with his back and inched up, he thought he would die. Despite his layers of shirts, the heat of her fingertips along his skin made him sizzle. He wanted to taste more of her sweetness badly, take more of what she had to offer, but he held himself in check. Just this earth-shattering kiss. Nothing more.

Right now, he needed to focus on the issues at hand. And for the moment, dealing with those unsavory guests was at the top of his list. He scanned the expansive lake before him.

He knelt as low as he could go, belly almost flat on the cold ground. He aimed his camera and snapped off several shots looking out across the lake's surface as the waves skipped along on top. Then he plunged another camera, a waterproof one, under the ice-cold water. He sucked in a harsh breath. Quickly, before he lost all feeling in his hands, he aimed blindly and shot views from multiple angles, from under the water, looking up to the surface.

Next, he withdrew from the bitter, cold water, deposited the camera behind a tree, and wrapped his arms around his middle in an attempt to warm them up as he figured out his next move.

Okay, the *Endeavor* went down in about five hundred and fifty to six hundred feet of water. The water was clear but incredibly cold. He needed to get down there and have a look around. He certainly could not do it as he was, with no scuba equipment, so that left one option. But what animal could withstand the cold, swim to that depth, and stay under long enough for a good search? And one that was native to around here, in case he was spotted?

Casting a look around, he stepped to a dead tree, its gnarled branches reaching pitifully out over the lake. But the trunk was wide enough to hide him and his clothes. Concentrating, he felt his teeth growing and fur spreading over his skin. Dropping to his hands and knees, he waddled over the rocks to the water, slipping into the cold lake, slapping the surface with his flat tail as he dove under.

As a beaver, he could easily navigate the rocks, logs, and debris in the lake. It was a maze of wrecked boats, fallen trees, and items lost from ships. Schools of fish darted out of his way. Heading straight out, he soon spotted the wreckage of the *Endeavor,* her name still legible, and he dove deeper. Paddling along the ship's bow, he came to the pilothouse. Twisting through the doorway, he found nothing of interest. Moving downstairs, he checked the crew's quarters, engine room, and finally the cargo hold. It was empty, a huge hole ripped in the side where she struck something on her way down. Maybe a chunk of ice or rocks. The cargo could have been manually moved through that hole.

Or it could have come loose during the rough winter months and shifted due to the strong lake currents. Exiting the hold through the hole, he searched the lake floor for foreign objects, using his front paws to shift rocks and weeds.

Nothing. No trace of anything. No signs that anyone had explored this area much. Whatever secrets the *Endeavor* had, she seemed determined to keep them. Finally, needing air, he swam up, popping to the surface and drawing in a big breath. There was no one in sight on the shore, so he paddled back to the dead tree.

—————

Raven knelt at the hearth, scooping a pile of broken China into a dustpan. The nerve of those ingrates breaking her China figurine. Robin had given her that for a birthday years ago.

Staring at the colorful, splintered pieces, she felt her shoulders sag. She'd already cleaned up so much, straightened a boatload of tossed-about items, and rehung the curtains they'd pulled off the wall for some reason. And she still had so much to do.

Next, she picked up books that had been tossed off the shelves. Most were old classics, some poetry books, and scores of books about boating and light-keeping facts and data. Somewhere along the line, newer books such as romances and mysteries gained a bit of shelf space.

Two different books caught her attention. Bound with

hard cloth covers and stitched with old string. Upon cracking open the cover, she scrunched her nose at the musty scent. These were *old* books. She gently touched the paper to turn the fragile pages. Pocket diaries. Dried flowers fell from one, and she quickly but gingerly scooped up the flowers. She sat on a chair she'd just upended, resting one book beside her and the other on her lap, and began randomly reading pages.

March 13, 1864, Mama doesn't even try to understand me. How can she expect me to not get bored and want to liven things up when each day stretches on like waves that crash ashore?

It was Madeline's diary before she died. Before she became the ghost Raven now knew. Her heart skipped a beat. Would Madeline mind if she read her old journal, her private thoughts when she was alive and a young girl?

May 4, 1864, Papa said he would let me and Henry take the rowboat out later this month, once it warmed up more. He is going to show us how to fish for the whitefish we all enjoy. Henry and I are already betting who can catch more.

She skipped a few pages ahead, and the flowery script suddenly stopped. Raven picked up the thicker notebook and turned to the first page.

Journal recordings of Ida Jacobson. Gull Island Light Keeper, along with husband John Jacobson and children.

The first entry was dated early 1857. In elegant calligraphic penmanship, Ida wrote of their first few nights on the island, how the children were settling in, and everyone's high expectations. Raven skipped ahead and found some entries specific to the challenges of their life and work presented. Friends and family who came to call. Wrecks that occurred, despite their dedication to keeping the light working night after night.

She found references to her children, especially Madeline, who grew from a young girl to a teenager on the pages. She appeared to be bright, mischievous at times, hard-working, and a bit of a dreamer. It seemed Madeline tested her parents' patience and pranked her siblings. She was the artistic one of the family as well.

She found an entry with sloppy writing, still in calligraphy, but not as carefully or thoughtfully written.

May 1864 John allowed Madeline and Henry to take the boat out to fish. They've done so a few times already. Today, the boat capsized. Before John or I could reach them, Madeline had drowned as she saved her younger brother. My wild, beautiful, impulsive daughter is dead. She was only sixteen. We buried her near the grassy pasture where the cows are kept. Henry is fine, but he feels guilty. I am grateful this horrible lake only took one of my children. I hate this lake, and I hate this island.

Raven paused, her hand over her heart as she absorbed the grieving mother's words. After that recording, entries became intermittent and shorter. Ida's whole outlook changed after she lost her daughter. Raven sincerely hoped she and the remaining family were able to get off the island soon thereafter.

She stood and took the books to the shelves. When time allowed, she'd read both, reading them slowly to understand their lives. Right now, she still had cleaning to finish before those miscreants returned. She resumed sweeping broken China. At least the two diaries were something good to come out of all this.

The closing of the front door brought her swiveling and sucking in a sharp breath. Who was returning?

"Hi, did you leave me any work to do?" Sebastian asked cheerfully.

She held out the dustpan, not quite sure what to do with it. "They made such a mess," she finished lamely. What prompted him to return and help? She expected him to be out taking his pictures and leaving her to her own troubles. This was not his problem. "Why are you doing this?" she asked curiously.

He blinked, pausing as he reached for the dustpan. "Why? Because it needs to be dumped out."

"No," she shook her head. "Why are you in here helping me?"

He shifted the contents of the pan, rattling them. "Oh, you mean instead of outside taking care of my business? Right? Maybe I decided my business can have more than just one point of interest." Walking away, he carried the dustpan to the kitchen trash can. She let out a breath and started lining books on the shelves in the living room. Behind her, he started sweeping the floor and shaking out rugs.

"I wonder where he is?" she said about ten minutes later.

"Where who is?"

"Salzburg. He hasn't come back yet."

"Salzburg? Oh, yeah, your dog. So he hasn't come back yet?" He paused as he wrestled the sofa back to where it belonged. "Oops, sorry, too many questions. I'll stop."

Somehow, his endless questions were not quite as bothersome as before. She replaced the rug that stretched along the front of the sofa, then moved to the window to look outside.

"I hope he's okay. What if Arthur found him while they were out digging up the island?" She had seen them leave with shovels and picks they found in the barn. A shudder ran over her. "I hate to think about what those tools in the wrong hands could do to a dog."

"I'm sure he's just fine and will be back soon. He sounds too smart to run off and not come back."

She turned as his hands came to rest on her shoulders. "He got separated from his original owners and never went back," she reminded him. "Do they mourn for their lost pet? Are they looking for him? Or had they given him up for lost?"

Sebastian gingerly stroked her cheek, setting off a series of heated explosions inside her. She trembled again, this time because of his touch.

"Your face reminds me of a rose," he whispered low. "Heart-shaped, petal-soft skin, rosebud, kissable lips, and deep, expressive eyes. You may have the temper of your namesake bird, Raven, but you are lovely as a blooming rose. You have such a good heart."

She balked under his lavish praise, dipped her head to the floor, and stepped away. Warmth spread over her face and down her neck. He captured her hands in his and rested his forehead against hers. Her pulse quickened at his intimate touch.

"I'm sorry if I embarrass you, Raven, but sometimes I can't help but say what I am thinking or feeling."

Heat and something stronger poured over Raven. She dared not risk looking upward to see his soulful eyes. Those bewitching green eyes. She might yield to the fire threatening to consume her. Overriding her intense passions, she struggled to regain her composure.

"That's very poetic, but I can't help but wonder about Salzburg."

"Maybe he just found something better here," he suggested, "and doesn't care to go back to his former life."

She heard the little sigh in his tone. "What do you mean?"

"He's got it made. I'm kind of jealous, actually."

Was he jealous of a dog? "How so?"

He smiled. "That dog gets to lie in bed next to you, listen to you talk, and sleep with you. He's a lucky hound."

Her mouth dropped open, and heat flooded her face. Indignant, she straightened her back. "And what makes you think all that?"

"Wow, what a transformation from rosebud to a raven right before my eyes." He moved to the sofa, sitting to study her with his arms spread along the back. She remained standing, lips pursed tight, arms folded, and waiting impatiently.

"Easy," he finally said. "All dogs will at least try to climb into their owner's bed. And you may be all prickly with me, but with someone you liked and trusted, I bet you'd warm right up. Like when you talk about your family or look at their photos, when you think I don't see you. Your face softens like butter and lights up like a Christmas tree. And you don't talk much to me, so I have to figure you'd pour your heart out to a dog that was willing to listen. A dog that was smart enough to be still and listen. Like I said, I'm kind of jealous."

Snatching one of the throw pillows, she tossed it at him. She marched from the room, filled with a mixture of embarrassment and, well, she didn't know. But his words rang a little too true for comfort.

She wrapped a scarf around her neck, threw on a jacket, and sauntered outside. She sat drawing her knees to her chest in the gazebo at the end of the porch. Resting her head on her knees, she stared at the water crashing onto the rocks and the gulls riding the air currents above.

Had she really been that prickly, as he called it, toward him? If she had, it was doubtlessly his fault. With all his questions, smiling charm, and determination to take pictures that would ruin her home.

Except she wasn't aware that he'd taken any pictures.

While he carried camera cases around, he had yet to carry one outside. Hope sprouted up within her.

Of course, he might not have had time to since the threesome had arrived and uprooted not only her life but his plans. She had to remember that in the short time he had been on the island, they had pretty much kept him hostage in one way or another. Closing her eyes, she tried not to think about last night or the boathouse. Or Helen with the missing tooth. Or what Arthur might yet decide to do to her. A shudder raced up her spine. If last night was any indication, they were both in serious trouble.

Chilled, she stood, stomping her feet and moving around the circle of the gazebo floor. How much different would things be between her and Sebastian if Arthur, Helen, and Dudley had not shown up? Remembering her naughty thoughts, she smacked her hand against the railing, muttering an oath. How much different did she want things to be between them?

If her body's heated response to his touch was any indicator, she was in trouble.

———

"I have a feeling your dog will be back soon," Sebastian said abruptly.

"You do? How?" Raven asked, setting her book down. She hadn't been reading it anyway.

They had eaten supper alone and were relaxing by the fire in the living room when Sebastian stated the declaration. The time spent had been quiet. They kept a measured distance from each other, and Raven sensed Sebastian's wariness and noticed how he kept watching the door. His constant guarding was playing on her nerves.

"It's getting late. He'll be tired from whatever he was

doing today. He'll probably want to come back and be looking for a warm bed to share." He cut a look at her. "Lucky dog," he muttered under his breath, but loud enough for her to hear.

"Arthur and the rest aren't back yet either," she observed, ignoring his look and suggestion. "Maybe they did get eaten by a bear." She could only hope.

He frowned. "I bet they will be back soon too. Sorry."

Silence fell between them. He stretched and yawned. "I think I'll turn in now, if you don't mind."

She did mind. Her pulse quickened at the thought of being left alone. She wanted him to stay with her. At least until Salzburg returned. If he returned. But that was also selfish of her. She would be okay, she assured herself. "Sure, that sounds fine. Goodnight."

Standing up, he stretched once more. "Goodnight, Raven. Sweet dreams."

She watched him climb the stairs, her heart growing heavier as he disappeared. Wanting so badly to hear whining or barking, or even a scratch at the door, she moved to the window and looked out. The full moonlight sparkled off the dark water and waves lapping onto the shore and bathed the light tower alabaster. It was as quiet outside as it was inside. Boards creaked overhead as Sebastian prepared for the night. She added another log to the fire, stepping back from the crackle and hiss.

Perhaps she ought to retire for the night. If she locked the door, would it keep her unwelcome guests out should they return? Probably not, she decided. They would simply break a window or bust down the door. Rather than risk damage to the house, she'd leave the door unlocked. Like she always had before all these people came thundering and blowing into her life like a wild nor'easter storm.

Checking once more for Salzburg, she slowly climbed the stairs.

———

Arthur, Helen, and Dudley arrived shortly after she went to her room. Arthur's thundering and bellowing travelled upstairs. Raven paused, heart skipping a beat and then thudding in her chest. She knew this house and could mentally track him from room to room as his stomping boomed, equal to her racing heart.

Doors slammed, and she jumped, dropping the books she had been shelving. Their thud upon landing was a pale comparison to the downstairs volume.

"Where is she?" he shouted. "That black-haired witch knows where my treasure is. She is going to show me. Right now," his continued yelling drew closer. "She left us to dig all over this island from one end to the other. The whole time, she's probably sitting here laughing at us. Now *I* want a good laugh. Where is she? By God, she'll give me the last laugh now."

Helen and Dudley joined in with their chorus of "Yeah," "You bet," and "Absolutely."

Raven waited inside her room with her fingers tightly curled into fists. *Fight or flight? This is my home. Fight!*

Arthur might kill her. She might kill Helen. She stepped to the hallway door; hand curled around the knob.

Cold sweat beaded on her brow, pooled at her breasts, and snaked down her back. Her heart raced. Ramped like a racecar.

Her breath came in short pants. Her weak knees trembled. She could only wait for him.

"I'll drag her out of her bed by her black hair. The witch," his yelling continued.

Heavy footsteps pounded up the steps, echoed by two more.

She was going to die. Or kill. Or both. Breath stalled. Sweat fell, chilling her.

A low snarl came from the hall.

She fumbled with the lock and the doorknob. The lock would never keep Aurther out. She peered through the one-inch opening.

Salzburg met Arthur at the top of the stairs, teeth bared, growling low and deep. Advancing one step, he barked twice, showing all his teeth. Ears back, he glared, as if daring Arthur to please come one step forward. Hackles rose along his shoulders. Gone was the soft and tender pet she shared her bed with last night. This dog was ready to kill.

Arthur stilled, blanching beneath his dirt-covered skin as he stared at the dog. At his sharp intake of breath, she suspected that if Salzburg attacked, his sheer size would probably force Arthur all the way down the stairs.

"Not now, dog," Arthur finally snarled, retreating down a step. "But later," he promised.

Only once Arthur reached the bottom step did Salzburg move. He lay at the top step, watching the landing of the stairs. Raven felt a stab of disappointment, hoping he would want to return to her. Yet this way, both she and Sebastian were protected. With Salzburg on guard, those people were going to spend the night downstairs.

She glanced at Sebastian's door, wondering why he wasn't checking on the situation. Surely, he couldn't help but hear the noise? Unless he was so exhausted, nothing could rouse him.

"Thank you," she whispered to the dog, who thumped his tail and flicked an ear toward her in acknowledgment, but did not turn his head.

Withdrawing to her own room, she drew up short, looking at a wisp of white standing and staring at Salzburg, her finger extended beneath her flowing gown.

Madeline.

CHAPTER
SIX

Sebastian met Raven as she exited her bedroom the next morning. Leaning against the wall, arms folded, watching the steps, he pushed off the wall at her approach.

"Morning," he greeted, offering her a tentative smile. "I heard the bellowing last night. When I came out, your pooch was already on guard. But I thought you might want me hanging around for a little while."

Grateful for his offer, she nodded. "Yes, that would be good. Where is Salzburg now?" *Had he already taken off?* She'd felt so safe knowing he was on alert and at the top of the stairs last night. Apparently, Sebastian felt the same way.

But now, with him gone again, and Arthur clearly thinking of revenge, she wasn't feeling safe. At least Sebastian was offering to stay with her. Glancing at him now, he looked more rested than he had yesterday.

"I'm not sure where he is," Sebastian answered.

She swept her hair into a loose braid, fidgeting. "You know, I've never been afraid to be here alone before," she said self-consciously.

"Well, you're not alone. And that is the problem. You're stuck with those three crazies. And me." Again, that lopsided smile knocked at her heart, untwisting a thread of doubt.

"I bet if you were alone, you would not be afraid. And besides, I'm a little scared to be around those three myself. Hard telling what they are capable of next."

Good point. In his case, Helen was the concern. His honesty disarmed her.

He caught her fidgeting hands. "Your braid is beautiful," he said softly. "I like your braids. Now, why don't you boil some of that coffee like you do, and we can talk. I won't leave your side, okay?"

Slipping downstairs with Sebastian, she found Arthur, Helen, and Dudley asleep, spread out on the chairs and sofas in the living room, snoring loudly. The fire was out. Their coats and outerwear lay scattered in a trail from the door to where they lay, mixed with dirt and melted snow. About to bend over to pick up their mess, Raven gave up with a heavy sigh.

"In time, we will all be gone," Sebastian whispered, gently pushing her toward the kitchen.

Wordlessly, she put the coffee on to boil and set out two cups. "Are you hungry?"

Leaning where he could watch both her and the doorway, he shook his head. "Just coffee for now."

Coffee finished boiling, they silently dressed in jackets, boots, and scarves, and headed for the gazebo.

"I really love this place," Raven said, sitting. "I especially like this gazebo."

Sebastian's gaze traveled the length of the shore, the light tower above them, and the tree line beyond. "So much great opportunity and I have yet to lift a camera to any of it," he said dreamily. "Why are you here, Raven?" he asked, swinging the conversation back to her. "Tell me in a way I can understand."

Her lips quivered, but she met his face. The breeze was already teasing her braid loose. His intense stare stopped her fidgeting fingers. Those green eyes, so patient. What harm was there in answering him? Like he said, soon he would be gone, out of her life. Only her heart was left to repair itself in the wake of the storm he was creating now.

An exhale to steady herself, she began, "I once had a husband and a successful career. Until he became jealous of it. He splashed false stories to create a scandal. I was dropped by my agent. Then my husband let me catch him in an affair. With my best friend."

Sebastian gasped at the sucker punch to his gut.

Raven blinked, shaking her head. "I'm not going to cry over them anymore," she declared, then continued stoutly. "So he sued for divorce. Because of the rumors and scandal he had started, he also sued for defamation of his character. He got the house, the money, pretty much all of it. He also got my friend."

"He's a rotten crumb ball, a low disgrace to manhood. He deserved the friend, and hopefully, he caught something terrible in the process."

Raven smiled. "Thank you, that's a very nice sentiment. I don't know about catching anything, but my lawyers got me a suitable alimony. Enough to support myself without having to return to work since no one was going to touch me right away. Not until the scandal died down. However, I still needed a place to stay short-term."

"Gull Island?"

"Yes, Wren is a commander in the Coast Guard, and he arranged it so that I can rent the light station using part of my alimony each month. In exchange, I keep the place in good condition."

"That sounds fair. Wren must be a good brother to pull strings like that for his sister. You said short-term. How long have you been here?"

"Five years."

"Five years? I was expecting you to say something like months. That's a long time, Raven. What do you consider a long-term residency?"

She took a swat at him and missed. "Once I got here, I just never wanted to go back. Wren comes a couple of times a month to bring me groceries and any mail I might get. I can call him if I need him in between. Just before she got pregnant, my sister came to stay with me for a short while."

"But you prefer to be here alone," he guessed, taking a drink of the cooled coffee.

"Yes."

"So, you've lived here for five years, with very limited twenty-first-century devices. What do you do all day, every day?"

She tinged, a brightness touching her cheeks. Did she dare trust him? To show him? Studying him, she thought he, of all people, might understand. Setting her cup down, she reached for his hand. "Come on, I want to show you something. It will answer your question."

Feeling the shared excitement in their touching hands, she led him along the porch, inside the house, quietly up the front steps, aware of the snoring trio in the rooms beyond, and up the stairs past her bedroom door.

Reaching another door, she paused, looking back at him, breath tight in her chest.

"Ready?" Her heart thumped.

———

Wordlessly, he nodded. *What could possibly be on the other side?* He swallowed hard.

She pushed the door open. Immediately, the smell of paints and turpentine inundated his senses. Stepping inside the room, he noticed stained drop cloths scattered on the floor. As he glanced around, he stilled with his mouth open.

Dozens upon dozens of paintings filled the walls and lined up in neat rows. He regained his composure and carefully crossed the room to slowly study them. They were all paintings of Gull Island, the lake, and her home. Studying the dates, some as old as five years ago, and some much more recent, he saw the progression of her talent. His artistic eye took in the depth of detail, the confidence of her strokes, and the bold flair in which she signed and dated each piece. She was a self-taught artist. A pair of oversized, black-rimmed eyeglasses lay on the paint table. He grinned, picturing them perched on her face when she painted. The image was provocative.

"My word, Raven, these are spectacular," he said, looking closely at one bearing a more current date. Something she had painted earlier in the year. It was like a photograph.

"I'm getting there."

Spinning back to her, he smiled. "Hey, I have some connections with the galleries. Do you have any idea what these would do if properly framed and displayed?"

"No, Sebastian." She shook her head. "You don't get it, do you? These are not for public display."

He frowned. "Then why are you bothering to paint them?"

"Because someday I will leave here, and I want to always remember how this place helped me."

Softly shaking his head, he said, "I still don't understand."

She moved to the newest work in progress, a stunning piece, and leaned against the wall. She let out a long breath, almost hurting him with the pain she experienced.

"When I first came here, I was broken, in heart and spirit. To say I was depressed would have been a huge understatement. To be honest, there were many times I stood on the widow's walk and contemplated simply going over the edge."

He gasped at the horror of the idea. He stepped toward her, but she held up a hand, stopping him.

"Wait. In time, I got over those ideas. Madeline helped a lot." She cracked a crooked grin. "Robin brought me a starter paint set, and one day, I was sitting in the gazebo with it unwrapped next to me. On a crazy impulse, I tore open the wrapper, set it up, and started slapping paint on the canvas. This is the result."

She lifted a small canvas from a drawer, holding it aloft. "Gull Island, Image Number One."

It was rough, he admitted, not unlike an amateur photographer who snaps pictures only to find them blurry or out of focus upon developing them. But clearly, she had learned the finer points of her art. And apparently, it had been the catalyst for her emotional healing. But how much had she really healed if she still preferred to be out here in the isolation of the island?

"So, if you have such a collection of these Gull Island paintings, why are you so against me taking photographs, which is essentially the same thing?"

She pushed her loosened braid back. "Because of what the final intention is to be. My paintings will never be seen by anyone, except perhaps one day by my sister and brothers. Your photographs, on the other hand, will be seen by hundreds, and maybe thousands. My paintings will never be the cause of people rushing the shore, stomping all over the place, and upsetting the cycle of life here."

"Like you feel my photographs will?"

She nodded.

"But, Raven, Gull Island is still owned by the Coast Guard. That makes it National property. People can't just gallop wildly over other Coast Guard-owned light stations."

"Oh, but in many cases they do. When there are no barriers or no people on hand to stop them, they arrive in cars and boats, set up picnics, and stomp all over, taking souvenirs that were never meant to be taken away. They break into the buildings, climb the light towers, sleep in the houses, have parties, and *always*, always leave their trash behind."

Deep in his heart, he knew that to be true. And she was just one woman, granted a very capable one, but she would be no match against boatloads of tourists eager to seek and explore the island. Just as she would be no match for any youthful groups with partying on their minds.

Not knowing what else to say, since they seemed to be on opposite sides of the matter, he changed the subject.

"Raven, I think your new guests downstairs are going to be growing more restless about this treasure thing. And more convinced you know how to lead them to it."

"But I don't," she persisted.

"Yeah, I believe you. But Arthur clearly doesn't. So be careful, okay. Especially when I or your dog aren't around. He just might get it in his irrational head to do something else rash and stupid."

Something he really would have to kill him for. Or Helen might get another crazy idea in her fool head, and it could complicate ways to protect Raven. Either way, he would feel better once those three were off the island for good. But then again, once they had a means off, it meant so did he, and Raven might send him packing as well.

"Just promise me, okay?" he implored.

"Of course, yes."

Thumping downstairs had them both looking for the door.

"Darn, they're waking up," she said. "Shame we don't have any sleeping pills. I could cook them a nice casserole laced with a triple dose. It was what a decent hostess should do, after all."

Chuckling, Sebastian drew her into his arms, inhaling deeply. Never mind the thudding of his own chest, her heart raced. For him? Or for concern about those downstairs?

———

It didn't take long for Arthur to confirm Sebastian's worst fears. Within minutes, he could tell by the bald man's angry gaze at Raven, he knew she knew where the treasure was and intended to make her tell him. His lecherous brow didn't help ease any of Sebastian's fears either. The man was trouble, and he'd bet anything today was going to be the day old Arthur snapped.

Dudley would be scared helplessly of a measly little bat, so that was good. He just followed orders but could be easily manipulated. And Helen, well, she was simply trouble. Despite his escape from the boathouse, she clearly had designs on him and was biding her time. Her roving eye confirmed that as well. Seemed he couldn't keep enough clothes on himself where that crazy broad was concerned. But he had learned she did not care for animals, especially big dogs. When Arthur went back downstairs, complaining and muttering about the dog upstairs, he had overheard Helen remind her brother how much she feared and hated dogs. It's wonderful to have gained even the smallest bit of information.

He could only hope the power came back soon today, and Raven could call her brother to get them off the island. Then he'd take his chances to hopefully stay and finish his job.

Coming around the corner of the stairs, Sebastian stilled at the sight. Standing a few feet away, watching him, was a ghostly, milky-white apparition.

"Uh, Madeline?" he asked, awkwardly. She appeared to be a teenage girl, dressed in a long velvet and lace dress, like something out of a *Gone with the Wind* movie set. She hovered a few inches off the ground, staring at him. Thrills shot through him. She seemed to be waiting. For what? He swallowed an unknown lump in his throat.

"Madeline, I know you've, uh, lived here a long time and you've no doubt come to know Raven pretty well. So, you have to believe me that I am only trying to look out for her. Honest, I am."

The girl tossed something from the folds of her gown to the floor. It slowly rolled toward him. He looked down and slowly back up to face the girl. A chill ran through him. The soup bone that Raven gave Sebastian in dog form sat at his feet. *She knows.*

———

Arthur and his companions once more were out prospecting for their treasure when Raven finished her breakfast. Sebastian, stating he wasn't hungry, said he had a quick matter to attend to and promised he would be right back. Thankful for a little time alone, and reasonably sure Arthur and company wouldn't be back too soon, she took her book and headed to the widow's walk of the tower to sit on the edge and read. The winds following the storm had died down enough to allow for a pleasant trip to the top again. And she loved to sit sometimes, with her legs dangling over the edge, and either read or stare at the mighty lake's surface.

She reached the top and stepped outside. The crisp October air swirled around her. The clouds shifted over-head, and the sun shone through. Leaning against the railing, she let the sun strike her face, enjoying the welcome warmth as it spread throughout her body.

It wouldn't be much longer before the power was restored again. Another day or two, maybe, and then she could call Wren to come and remove her unwanted guests. With any luck, it might even be as soon as today.

But did that include Sebastian? He had yet to take the photographs he came for. So, was he willing to go without them? It didn't sound like he had much choice. And did she really want him to go? Despite her talk with him earlier about liking to be alone on the island, his presence had awoken something inside her that dared to say otherwise. Something that dared her to deny its whispered suggestions that she might really be falling for him. She giggled. Too late, she'd already fallen for him and his bewitching green eyes, crooked smile, and tender touch. That internal voice dared her to say she didn't want him to stay, but as more than a guest. Her heart leapt and beat fast. She wanted him to stay as her man.

"There she is. Up there," Arthur's angry bellowing reached her.

Dropping the book, she scanned the rocky ground. Standing below, waving a short-handled pickaxe at her, Arthur beat his fist in the air. Dudley and Helen stood nearby, also holding out shovels. Cold fear crawled up her spine at the sight. A sweat broke on her forehead. Pulse racing, she realized she was trapped at the top with no way down but through them.

"She's gonna show us that treasure, and right now! Let's go get her," Arthur barked, waving his axe like a club. "I want that black-haired witch!"

Oh Lord, where was Sebastian? Standing, she considered her options. There was no lock on the light tower. She could never run fast enough to outdistance the three of them. Trapped like a rat, she could only wait. *Could I push them over the railing? Would I have the guts? To shove another human to their death?* Her stomach flipped. Her throat tightened.

Madeline materialized beside her, pointing to draw her attention to the house. Trembling, Raven gripped the rail and looked over the edge.

Could a ghost scare them away?

"G-g-go after them, Madeline," she stuttered. "You might be the only thing they fear."

Maybe.

Madeline raised her arm to point to the house once more, then slowly faded. Raven was alone.

Barking reached her ears as Salzburg broke through the trees at the corner of the house, where Madeline had pointed. The sleek German Shepherd raced for the trio. He showed his white teeth and long fangs. His growl seemed to reverberate up the tower to Raven.

Her hand pressed to her mouth in horror. The railing dug into her belly.

Salzburg leaped through the air, aiming straight for Arthur. The big man beckoned to the dog, muttering words lost in the wind. Salzburg latched onto Arthur's right arm, his weight swinging Arthur half around.

The man roared in pain. He shook his arm, and Salzburg rolled across the ground before springing to his feet.

He sprinted toward Dudley, who had taken a step toward him. The man visibly trembled but still held his shovel aloft.

Salzburg snapped his jaws, clicked his teeth with his ears laced back. He barked a deep warning.

Screaming like a girl, Dudley dropped his weapon and ran for the shelter of the barn.

Helen dropped her shovel and followed, shrieking as well. They disappeared inside the barn after closing the door behind them.

Raven cheered Salzburg for his bravery and success. Her fist punched the air.

"Yay, Salzburg!"

Salzburg whirled around, redirecting his focus to Arthur with a low growl and advancing a step.

"Come on, mutt, it's time. Just you and me." He stood, legs apart, braced. "And then I'm gonna get that witch and drag her by that black hair until she gives me my treasure."

"No," she shouted. Her words ripped into the wind.

Swinging his pickaxe in the air awkwardly in his left hand, he swung at the dog. Salzburg deftly darted out of the way, charging in with a fierce bark, only to dance out of the way as Arthur stepped closer.

"Come on, you mangy mutt, hold still." He swung blindly, missing with each swipe.

Salzburg barked once, leaping into the air, and connected with his right arm again. Arthur went down under his weight. As he sank to his knees and spun halfway around, he still managed the feat of lifting his axe and letting it fall.

"No! No! Damn you!" Her words would never reach Arthur way down there, but she screamed them regardless. Fear tore at her as she helplessly watched. Her stomach clenched.

Yelping suddenly, Salzburg released Arthur's arm. He rolled over, springing up on three legs, holding the front leg up to dangle uselessly. There was a gash from the axe.

Arthur lay on the ground, rocking and screaming in pain as he cradled his arm. Blood shone through his coat sleeve.

"Cursed mutt," he swore loudly at the dog. "Cursed mutt."

Salzburg, ears still back, lifted his menacing lips in a snarl. Beside him, Madeline formed with her arms raised high.

Arthur shrieked, scooting away from the dog and the ghost.

Madeline drifted to the barn, her white dress grazing the snowy ground. She passed through the wooden door. From inside, Raven heard the screams of terror.

Salzburg limped painfully forward to the light tower and gazed up to where Raven stood, still leaning out along the rail. Wagging his tail once, he slowly hobbled over the ground back to the trees alongside the house, back where he came from.

"Wait, Salzburg, don't go," she yelled, whirling away from the railing. She raced down the steps, taking them in twos. Reaching the bottom, she flung the door open. The dog was gone.

"Don't go," she called into the wind. Racing past Arthur, she ran to the corner of the house. Slamming to a halt, her heart sank. He was gone. Hand to her chest, she fought for breath, sucking in lungfuls of cold air. Then she noticed a few drops of bright blood staining the rocks.

She followed the splatters and spots to where they disappeared into the tree line of the woods.

Anger boiled within her. Raw anger. Almost a murder lust. Spinning around, she stormed in the direction of

Arthur first. She kicked the pickaxe and shovels from his reach and stood there, hands on her hips, glaring at him.

"Aren't you gonna help me?" he demanded. "A ghost nearly killed me. Your ugly damn mutt attacked me. I might get rabies now."

If only.

"Serves you right if you did get killed or rabies," she retorted, raising her voice and speaking with conviction. "I have no intentions of helping you. Get off my island. Swim if you must."

She snagged one of the shovels and marched to the barn. Though there were no more screams, she could hear heavy breathing, loud whispers, and shuffling beyond the door. Madeline had left as easily as she had entered once her task was done. Sliding the handle of the shovel through the door handles, she smiled in tart satisfaction.

Dudley and Helen would have a hard time getting out of there now. Served them right as well. She rubbed her hands together, feeling no pity for any of them. Maybe Madeline would return while they were trapped.

Now to find Salzburg and Sebastian.

CHAPTER
SEVEN

An hour passed before Sebastian returned. Coming from behind the boathouse, he walked slowly across the rocks, coming to a halt when he spotted Arthur. The man had managed to pull himself to a sitting position and cradled his arm close to his chest.

"That black-haired witch's mutt attacked me," Arthur declared. "You gotta shoot him. He's got rabies or something. And a ghost tried to kill me. This place is haunted," he exclaimed.

"If Raven's dog attacked you, it was because you deserved it, not because he has rabies. And ghosts don't kill people. What were you doing?"

"Nothing," he declared boisterously.

"Looks like I missed a good fight," he said. "Where are the other two?"

He cast a scowl in the direction of the barn. Sebastian followed his gaze, noting the shovel's handle barring the door. A grin split his lips.

"I see. And where did Raven go?"

Arthur sneered, refusing to answer. Sebastian pushed him with his boot. Arthur howled, rocking on the ground.

"I'm dying here and you're kicking me."

Sebastian bit back a sigh of impatience. He had hoped he would return and find Raven waiting nearby. While the treasure hunters were out of the fight, it didn't ease his concern for where she might have gone. "I am not playing games with you," he warned. "And if you don't cooperate, you'll see what a real kicking is. Now, where is she?"

"That way." He muttered, swinging his head to the trees and hills beyond the house.

Fear pulsed through him. Why would she go up there? Then he knew. To find her dog. Leaving the others, he broke into a run up the hill. He considered shifting to something swifter, with a strong sense of smell to track her down, then reconsidered. He needed to be human when he found her. Because he was going to find her.

———

Raven slowed down, holding her side and catching her breath. He was truly gone. Even on three legs, he'd vanished into the thick woods and silently disappeared. He was probably never coming back.

And now she had Arthur and the others to deal with. But where was Sebastian?

"Sebastian," she shouted once more. Her calls for both of them had been fruitless for the last half mile she'd climbed the inner terrain.

"Raven. Here, over here," Sebastian's voice rang out through the trees.

She watched as he came around a thick spruce tree large enough to hide a bear. Just seeing him striding toward her, she couldn't stop the eager thrill racing through her. He was back. They were safe. She stretched out her arms and slid into his welcoming embrace.

His hands cradled her to his chest, where his heart beat reassuringly in her ear. His voice rumbled softly. "What happened? Why are you up here?"

Tears gathered in her eyes. "Oh, Sebastian, that wicked Arthur slashed poor Salzburg with the pickaxe. He hobbled away on three legs. He probably crawled off to the woods to die now. I can't find him," she sobbed with the hot tears streaming down her cheeks.

"Whoa, easy there," he said. He rubbed the moisture away with his thumbs. "He's a smart dog. He knows how to take care of himself."

"But he's wounded," she defended.

"I bet that old dog has been through worse before and still survived."

"But his leg was practically cut in two!" New sobs shook her. Had he not been holding her, her weak knees would've failed, and she'd be a pile on the ground.

———

"Come here, Raven." Speaking low, he gathered her close, head cradled to his chest. Her chest rose and fell against his as she fought the sobs within. His heart melted like butter. She had gotten attached to that dog. What if he never came back?

"Honey, maybe it's possible Salzburg was here only to serve a purpose. You know, to protect you from those three troublemakers. Now that the danger seems to be gone, he might know he's no longer needed."

"Sebastian! How can you say that?" She tried to draw away from him, but he refused and held her steadfast.

"I just think it's a good idea to entertain the idea that he was only here temporarily. I know you kind of loved him and all, but..."

Her cries stopped his words. Falling silent, he eased her back to a large rock where he sat, bringing her with him. He held her close as the sobs rocked her body. Waiting it out, gently rocking her, he closed his eyes, wondering what would happen if the dog never returned. Gradually, her sobs relented, finally slowing to hiccups.

"Guess what? I met Madeline earlier."

"How did that happen?" her muffled voice asked.

"I was upstairs at the time, and she just appeared. She doesn't seem to have a lot to say, does she?"

"I've never heard her speak."

"It was my first encounter with a ghost. Kind of nifty, I guess."

"She came and helped Salzburg fight Arthur and the others. She gave Helen and Dudley a good scare inside the barn." She chuckled.

"I wish I could have seen it."

She drew back, and this time he let her go. Wiping at her eyes, she left a wet trail. "You should have seen how she scared Arthur. I bet you didn't believe me when I first told you about her," she accused.

He grinned. "Honestly, no, I didn't. I thought you were making up a ghost story to keep me in line or something."

"Ha," she said in tart satisfaction. "In that case, I'm glad you finally met her."

"Yeah, me too."

She withdrew her hand. "Sebastian, you're bleeding." She stared at the bright blood on her fingers and rubbed two fingers together. Immediately, she began feeling around his jacket sleeve. "What on earth happened to you?"

Gingerly, he pulled away. "Nothing. No big deal. I slipped and fell on the rocks. Got a little cut, is all."

"Oh, we have to go to the house, and right now. I need to look at that."

"Raven, it's not..."

Standing, she wordlessly pointed down to the house.

"All it needs is a couple of bandages. I can do that myself. You don't need to trouble yourself. Really."

"Now. Or else I'll get Madeline out here to help me."

He paused, wondering if she and the ghost had that sort of relationship. He warily eyed her. It was possible. He surrendered, blowing out a deep sigh. He wasn't sure how this was going to go off, but he would bet it was going to be bad.

"What about him?" he asked as they entered the yard, almost in desperation, nodding out to where Arthur swayed, still cradling his arm.

She waved him off without so much as a glance. "He can rot for all I care."

Apparently, concern for her injured pet and him had not dimmed her feisty temper. Or maybe it made it worse. Once inside, he settled on the chair she pulled out for him. He winced while shrugging free of his jacket.

"So how did you manage to trip and fall on the—Oh my word." She stepped back, wide-eyed and staring at his arm. She opened her mouth to speak but said nothing.

Like a fish out of water, gasping.

Holding his arm, blood saturating his shirt sleeve, he had dread in his heart. "It's really not as bad as it looks." Even his voice held a measure of dread and false optimism.

Creeping forward, tentatively touching him, she couldn't withhold the pinch of pain from her face. "You are going to need stitches at the very least. Probably more than that. Certainly, more than I can do here." She rushed and grabbed a towel from the rack by the stove.

He shook his head, feeling the pain and hating himself for it. "Just wrap a bandage around it and it should be fine for now."

Liar.

"Hold that for pressure," she instructed, placing the towel over the wound and then resting his good hand on top of the towel. With a pair of scissors, she cut his shirt below the shoulder.

"I wish you wouldn't do that."

"It's just a shirt. It will have to be cut off eventually."

He looked away, waiting. It wasn't the shirt that he worried about.

Her fingers gingerly worked to peel the sleeve from his arm when she stopped. He turned to face her as she lifted a small section with a fingernail. The color drained from her face as she studied the clean, deep cut. It had gone straight through close to the bone.

"How exactly did you get this? And are you hurt anywhere else you haven't bothered to mention?"

He grinned at the hint of sarcasm in her tone. Even concerned about him, Raven was still Raven. "No, that's it. Honestly, if you just slap a bandage on it to hold it—"

"Sebastian," she raised her voice, edging her derision toward anger. "Your arm is practically cut in two! Just like Salzburg's. It needs a whole lot more than—" Her words died off as she stared at him. Her eyes widened. He swore he could see her thoughts slowly shuffling themselves into place in her mind. This is what he really had wanted to avoid.

Too late now, Knight. Time to deal with the consequences. You should have been more careful.

"No." She breathed, backing up, her hand to her mouth. "Tell me what happened to you," she demanded.

"I was walking on the shore and tripped. I hit a sharp rock."

"I don't believe you."

He heaved a deep breath. Oh, but she was going to lose it now.

"Okay, you want the truth? I'll show it to you. But remember, you asked for it."

Concentrating, the bracelet sizzled, his ears stretched up, his nose grew out, rounding in shape, his teeth lengthened, and the fur pushed along with whiskers. At her horrified gasp, he stopped and moved to reverse the process.

Stumbling backward, fist to her mouth, she landed against the wall. Standing there, she stared at him as though he were an alien. "Who are you?" she finally managed to ask, croaking like a frog. "What are you?"

If he could, he would've held her tight in his arms. But her horrified, gasping, bug-eyed expression proved she wouldn't allow it, and his arm wouldn't either. Shrugging, he explained. "I'm Sebastian, the same man who has been on this island with you for days. And I'm also your canine pal, Salzburg. I'm a shapeshifter."

———

Raven aimed for the nearest chair, catching herself before hitting the floor. She hoisted herself onto the seat cushion and kept a good distance between them. Her heart was beating as if it was going to bust through her chest. Her hands trembled. Her lips worked to suck in a ragged breath, then another. Suddenly cold and in shock, she rubbed her arms. What had she seen? What had he just said?

She shook her head. No, no, no.

"Explain," she demanded as her knees quaked. She had not seen what she just thought she saw. No way had he almost turned into a dog. There had to be some other explanation.

"Well, ah, remember when I told you about that year I spent with the Native American tribe some time ago? Well, it started then. It's this bracelet that allows me to change shapes. The medicine man gave me the bracelet. The bracelet gives me the power."

"How?" Doubt, suspicion, and confusion all rushed to fill the single word. She had no clue how she felt about...any of this.

"I don't really know. Magic of some sort. All I know is that the medicine man told me to never take off the bracelet. If it ever came off, the magic would be broken, and I would be forever stuck in whatever form I was in at that time."

She remembered the first time she met Salzburg and how he pulled away when she tried to check for ID. Had that bracelet changed into a collar of sorts?

"What does that bracelet do when you..." Words failed her. At least she wasn't stuttering. Not yet anyway. Her heart was certainly skipping along at an irregular rhythm. And her mind wrestled to make sense of this impossibility.

"When I shift? It stretches or shrinks to fit around whatever animal I am shifting into. Collars, halters, leg bands, whatever. And back again later to this. It's all part of the magic."

"How do you..."

"Shift?" He grinned slightly, apparently at her inability to say the word. "Easy. I just picture the animal I want to shift into, and gradually, I feel the change take place. It only takes a few moments. And then when I want to return to my human form, same thing, just imagine me and presto."

"That's how you escaped the ropes when you were tied up?" she guessed.

"Twice. Here in the house and once in the boathouse. A cougar the first time, a bird the second."

"Cougar?" She felt a shiver at the word, remembering Dudley's remark about seeing one.

"I ran out to the barn, thinking you might need some protection. I barely got back in and dressed before you all caught me."

Gut churning, she processed what he was saying. It was a lot to digest. She balled her fists into her lap to stop the trembling. She eyed him, finding it hard to breathe, having to remember to breathe. This was impossible.

But she saw it. She saw him...shift.

"You're Salzburg?" she asked. At least her voice no longer croaked. Slowly stitching the pieces together, frustration ruled.

"Well, technically, he's me. I just shifted into his form."

"So, when Arthur cut Salzburg's leg with the ax, he really..."

"He really cut mine," Sebastian nodded to his arm. "And it hurts regardless of what form I'm in."

She fell silent, thinking again. "So, when you're...shifted or whatever, do you understand everything you see and hear like a person would? Do you remember it all after you've...returned?"

He hesitated. Wearily, he lowered his gaze. "Yes."

———

The transformation was instant. Color flooded her cheeks as rage filled her eyes. Sucking in a deep breath, he steeled himself against her and her anger.

Drawing herself from the chair, she stood over him. "How dare you try something so low-handed. You deceived me, Sebastian Knight," she yelled.

"I did it to protect you," he countered.

"You listened to everything I said about you, private

stuff, and you never once said a thing," she said with clenched fists.

"How could I? I was a dog."

She raised a hand as though to slap him. If he were not injured, with his arm half hanging off, she probably would have.

"That night, when I thought Helen was playing her hanky-panky games with you in the boathouse, having her wicked way with you, you were really in my bed. Oh my. You even watched me strip and take a bath." Tears filled her eyes.

"I looked away, at the door, if you recall. I remained a gentleman. Even in dog form."

She snorted before continuing to scold him. "You still deceived me. You could have told me the next day who you were. But you did not. You even asked me where my dog was when you knew all along."

"I thought it seemed more credible that way. For you to think you really had a big canine protector. I am sorry."

She flung her hands at him with a tart laugh as he ducked. "If you had been honest with me in the first place, there would never have been a need to be credible. You still lied to me. So don't tell me you're sorry now."

"I am sorry. You don't believe it, but I am sincerely sorry for misleading you. But it was the only way I could get close enough to you to protect you from Arthur. You would have never let me, as Sebastian, that close to you, and you know it, Raven." He ached for her anger, knowing it was his fault. He wanted to apologize, take her in his arms, and kiss her tears away. Instead...they had this.

"Maybe not. But there had to have been a better way."

"There might have been, but I sure couldn't think of one. And now I think you love that dog more than you care about me."

About to retort, she closed her mouth instead. Whirling around, she raged to the end of the room and back again, arms flailing the air as words failed her.

She looked like a little tornado. He was almost amused by the sight. Too bad it was all aimed at him.

"At least now you know he didn't crawl off to die," he said gently.

"Too bad," she snapped while pulling a small box from atop a shelf. She slammed it on the table, yanked, and spilled first aid supplies. "There is nothing in here adequate to fix your arm," she said, rifling through the meager selection of bandages, antibiotic ointment tubes, and gauze.

"How about a couple of sticks?"

"To beat you with?"

Her face and tone remained deadpan. Her anger was winding down slowly, but he was sure she'd smack him with a stick if she could.

"Ha. No, to use as a splint. To hold the loose flaps of skin together until we can get real help. And some aspirin or something if you have that around the place."

Her breathing slowed, no longer heaving in her rage as she stood back, studying him with a little tilt to her head. "You do look pale," she observed. "I have some sturdy dowel rods that might work as a splint. And some pain relievers. Hang on."

———

Stopping at the bottom step with her hand on the banister, she turned to face him with a fluttering heart.

"Did I snore?" She hated herself for asking but could not stop the words tumbling from her lips.

"What?"

"At night, when Salzburg, I mean you, were in bed with me, did I snore?"

He gave her a tight smile. "No. But you did do this cute little whimpering thing."

She frowned, not finding that description amusing. Or especially flattering.

"I figured it meant you were having good dreams," he explained. "Probably about me."

Sending him a dark scowl, she barely resisted the impulse to throw something at him. For his conceit and his deception. How dare he.

Leaving him, she ran upstairs to her bedroom. Gathering the items, she took a moment to sink to the bed, pressing her hand to her stomach. She really did see him change into Salzburg. Right? And he admitted it. Oh, heavens above, this was unbelievable. She didn't know what to think right now. Sebastian's comments whirled through her mind, not making any sense. A shapeshifter? Good heavens.

But right now, he was also injured. Apparently injured while protecting her from Arthur's advance up the tower to get her. Doubtlessly, the lunatic was going to really harm her. She supposed she owed Sebastian some measure of decency for that sacrifice.

Sucking in a deep breath, she picked up the rods and bottle of pain reliever and headed back downstairs. He was dozing in the chair. Slowly approaching him, there was the same tug in her heart like the time she watched him on the gazebo playing his saxophone. That untying of the heartstrings, the walls of resolve crumbling, that increasing flutter of hope as the knots holding it captive slowly came undone.

"Sebastian?"

He roused, blinking at first. "So, you're not going to

beat me over the head with those after all? You just missed your chance if you were."

"Not yet. I might if you keep asking so many questions. Now, can you help me do this?"

As they were finishing their joint coordination of applying the bandages, the lights flickered and turned on. The refrigerator hummed.

"Hey, how about that. You have power again."

"Yes." She breathed a sigh of relief. "Finally." Going to the phone, she immediately dialed her brother's cellphone. Her heart hammered as she counted rings. *One. Two. Three.*

"Wren? It's Raven," she gushed when she heard his cordial hello. "We just got power back. I need you to come out here right away. Immediately." She emphasized the urgency. "There are two injured...people here." She cast a look at Sebastian. "And three that need to be arrested. Bring some officers with you." She ended the call, hands shaking. Only then did she realize she had never let her brother speak a single word.

"I'm still a person, Raven," Sebastian said softly as he met her eye.

"You also admitted to being a cougar and a bird. And Salzburg." She looked away. "What else have you been while you were here?"

He shrugged and blew out a long breath. "A beaver. I had to go out to the *Endeavor* and look around. That seemed like a good way to get there and back."

"That damned boat." She gritted her teeth. "I am sorry to have ever heard about it. Stupid thing has been nothing but trouble."

"Not the boat's fault for sinking, Raven. Blame Arthur and his crazy scheme to get rich."

"Did you find that treasure while you were out there? Did you find the boat?"

He nodded. "I found the boat, but her cargo seems to want to remain a mystery. There was no trace of it."

Slipping back into her chair, she took the top off the bottle of pills. Shaking two out, she recapped the bottle. "Would you like some water?"

At his nod, she rose, brought him a glass, and sat down, resting her hands on her lap.

"I don't know what to think," she said quietly, watching him take the medicine.

He nodded. "I really do wish I could have spared you this. I wish I could help you process it somehow. I know it's a lot."

"Who else knows you can...do this?"

"Not too many people. For obvious reasons. So, how long until your brother gets here?"

Not soon enough, but she wasn't about to tell him that. "You know Wren is going to insist you go to the mainland for treatment," she pointed out instead.

"Yeah, I figured he will. So, will I be welcomed back, Raven?"

She slapped the table with her palms. "You can't ask me that now. Not after what just happened."

An uneasy and thick silence fell between them at her outburst.

"Look," he said at last, easing out a heavy breath. "I never meant to deceive you. Or hurt you. I was only doing what I could to keep you safe. If those three never showed up here, or were decent when they had, I would never have had to shift."

Interesting point. And then she would have still fallen in love with him and never known about his secret. So, should she be happy about this or not?

The door banged. Her head shot up.

"Look out," she shouted, rushing to her feet. The chair slid back to the wall, and she pointed in alarm. No....

Sebastian whirled in the chair.

Arthur lurched, face compressed, arm oozing blood, hand outstretched, holding a rusty shovel up.

"You and your cursed dog and meddling boyfriend. I'm getting that treasure," he snarled. "You're coming with me, woman. Your wretched ghost be damned," he bellowed. His eyes were insane, crazed. Glassy red.

She staggered against the wall. Her chest tightened. Her heart pumped spasmodically. She held her breath.

Sebastian launched and kicked away from the chair. Halfway through the air, his clothes fell away, revealing a shiny black and brown fur coat and sharp, bared teeth. His jaws wrapped around Arthur's wrist. He pushed his weight into the man's chest with a hard growl.

They landed on the floor, skidding across the hardwood, pushing rugs in front of them. Salzburg was on top of Arthur, biting hard and refusing to let go.

They slid to the bookcase, a heavy mahogany antique piece. Arthur's head struck the corner. He stilled and groaned softly.

Their enemy down and out, Salzburg rolled off and lay still on the floor, his maimed front leg hanging uselessly. He raised his head, only for it to fall to the floor with a weary moan.

Raven stared, first at the pile of clothes that had pooled at her feet, then at the unconscious Arthur with two arms bleeding, and then at the shovel that had gone flying against the wall.

"Salzburg," she screamed when she finally looked at the dog. She rushed to him and knelt to cradle his silken head on her lap.

"Sebastian," he corrected as the shift took place. Still

lying on the floor, naked and bleeding, he rolled his eyes up to Raven. "I'm Sebastian. Though I think it's Salzburg you love more than me."

Horrified, she scooted back. One moment, she was speaking to green-eyed Sebastian, the next second, Salzburg was flying through the air to attack Arthur. One minute, she was cradling Salzburg's silken head with soft brown eyes in her lap, and then he became Sebastian with those damn intense green eyes.

"I don't understand," she faltered, looking at the naked man.

"It's not something meant to be understood." His breathing was labored, causing him to speak slowly. "It's the magic from that medicine man. It's all I can explain. Can you please help me get my clothes back on? And maybe re-bandage my arm?"

She could not reconcile the image of the furry dog and the naked man in her mind. Grimly, she stuck to the task. It was a struggle, but she managed to get him dressed. She could see the weariness pulling at him, and she hastened to bring the supplies to him to re-bandage his arm. Resignedly, he closed his eyes and submitted to her ministrations.

Where fur once was, skin was once again. She touched him gingerly. Normal, warm human male skin. Maybe a little too warm, she worried.

Hearing a boat outside, she breathed a sigh of relief. Wren.

Within moments, followed by several of his officers, Commander Wren Koynes burst into the room. Glancing around in wide-eyed disbelief at Arthur moaning his way back to consciousness, the shambles of the room, over-turned chairs, and Raven on the floor next to Sebastian.

He asked her, "Rave, what the devil happened here?"

"Arrest him," she said, pointing to Arthur. "There are

two more in the barn that need to be arrested too. They were after the cargo on the *Endeavor*. They've been horrible to us and digging up half of Gull Island."

"There are so many rumors about what happened to that shipment that no one knows the true story." Her brother shook his head.

"There's treasure here on this island," Arthur insisted with a slur, while suspiciously eying them all. "And she would've shown me where if it hadn't been for her cursed dog and trained spook attacking me. I want that dog shot."

Wren turned to Raven with his eyebrows raised. "Dog?"

She cast an uneasy glance at Sebastian sitting on the floor. "Well, a dog swam ashore right after the storm. I sort of adopted him since he hung around. But he did protect me from Arthur." She peered in Sebastian's direction. "I don't know where it went though. Last I saw, he was heading up into the hills."

"She lies! It—"

"Petty Officer, arrest that man," Wren commanded, waving to Arthur. "You three, go find the ones in the barn and arrest them too." He waved to the officers crowding the doorway.

Climbing to her feet, she hastily told him the highlights, skipping uneasily over Sebastian's unusual skill.

He stepped over the rubble to assist Sebastian to his feet. "You need medical care, Mr. Knight. We'll take you in right away.

Sebastian wearily eyed her brother. "Commander, Raven—"

"I'll stay here with Raven. Petty Officer, help Mr. Knight to the boat and make him comfortable. Ensure he receives care first upon arrival at port. Send another boat back for me."

Matters handled and orders given, he guided Raven to a

chair and gently nudged her onto one. It felt good to hand over control to Wren for now. She silently watched the men escort Sebastian and Arthur from the house. She held Sebastian's gaze for a lingering moment. Her chest tightened. What to say? Not good-bye. She was sure he would return. Then what?

After all this, all they shared, would he still take his photos?

CHAPTER
EIGHT

The scent of apples and spice did nothing to perk her up. Raven dutifully took a sip from the steaming cup but set it aside, ignoring the look of worry lining Wren's brow as he returned to his chair. Guilt at knowing he worried for her nipped at her like a persistent dog. *Oh, bad analogy.*

She wished she knew how to alleviate Wren's worry and her guilt. Both tasks seemed impossible. She nibbled her lip to keep from crying.

Maybe her shock was settling in.

"Rave, why don't you go stay with Robin for a bit?" he suggested softly as he reached for her hand. "You had a lot tossed at you in the last couple of days. Maybe you need to get off the island for a little while."

She shook her head, but he held up a hand to halt her protest. "You could help her paint and get ready for that little one they're expecting."

"The last thing Robin and Ricky need is me underfoot. This is my home, Wren, and I will stay here."

He set his teacup aside. "Okay. The lights are flashing in your eyes, your jaw is jutted out, and I know better than to argue with you like that." He shook his head. "Though I would still think you couldn't get away from here fast enough, at least for a little while. But that's just my thinking, and even as kids, we thought differently."

"Thank you for understanding."

He chuckled, giving another shake of his head. "Never said I did. However, once I return to port, I need to officially book those three characters on multiple charges, as many as I can think up between now and my return."

Raven tried the tea again, this time tasting the rich spices. "You always did make good tea, Wren."

"What about Sebastian Knight?"

"What about him?" Did she just bristle upon hearing his name?

"For starters, what was his role in all of this adventure?"

She hesitated the briefest of moments. "I told you. He protected me, keeping Arthur away."

"I owe the guy a debt of gratitude for that. Seems he had his hands full with the crazy sister. I need to add kidnapping to the list of charges if Knight wants to prosecute."

"Yes. Seems he never had a chance to take any of the photos he came to take."

"So will he now, once he returns, after everything that has happened?"

"I'm not really sure." She drew imaginary circles in the lace tablecloth with her fingertip.

"Anything else?"

"Like what?" She brushed her hair away, not liking the curiosity on his face.

"Rave, I noticed that look you gave Knight on his way out. I've only seen that look in your eye one other time. It was a long time ago."

"Wren—"

"You were a young girl, very much in love. It was a beautiful look on you then. I never thought I'd see it again."

"Wren," she warned.

"I just want to know if Knight put that look there. Because it kind of looks like it from my point of view."

"What would it matter?"

He rested his hand on top of hers. "Because then I'd like to thank him if he had."

———

Raven sighed. The house was quiet. The kind of quiet she had known before the storm blew in with its group of travelers. Yet somehow it was different than before. Wren had left. She managed a light meal and decided a bath was in order. First, a real shower to scrub away the assorted feelings she had experienced over the last few days. Feeling them flowing down the drain, she gave a name to each one, letting them go. Anger, fear, worry, surprise, shock, and horror were just a few.

Next, filling the antique claw-foot tub with a silky bubble bath, she slid into the welcoming warmth, letting it envelop her in its peace and softness. Leaning onto the bath pillow, she closed her eyes and played back the last few hours in her mind.

How would things have been any different had she never known about Sebastian's unique ability? Despite her unwillingness to name why the house felt different tonight, she knew. Because neither Sebastian nor his dog form was nearby. For the first time in five years, she felt utterly alone, not just on the island, but in the world.

———

Sebastian fretted under the confines of the infirmary. He was ready to go, but they insisted on keeping him overnight. It seems they were worried about infection or some such nonsense and claimed he needed antibiotics and fluids. He reluctantly agreed to pacify them. Now he regretted it.

Tossing and turning restlessly on the uncomfortable bed, he thought of the big canopy bed in Raven's house. Though he barely used it, it called to him.

Who was he kidding? It wasn't that bed, or the room, or that entire place that called him. It was the woman he had left behind. For the first time in his memory, he had no great itch to grab his cameras and snap photos of nature at her glory, best or worst. To be honest, as he flipped over again, the only itch he had right now was to get back to Raven.

Ah, but what kind of reception would she give? Prickly like usual? Or worse, now that she knew about him? He'd never forget that uneasy look that passed between them as he was taken away. She had wanted to say something. What had it been?

Come back soon? Or go to hell?

He hoped for the former but suspected it might have been the latter.

Pounding the pillow into a shapeless mass, he considered his options. He could return to the island, shoot the shots per the contract, maintain a distance between them if she wanted it that way, and take his leave once he was finished with the assignment. That might be the best option. He may discover what the allure and mystery of the island were that way, whatever it was that set it apart as special.

Of course, there was the other option of returning, taking enough pictures to satisfy his contractual obligation and keep the peace with his boss, and lingering on. He could tell Raven how he really felt, all mushy and gushy whenever he thought about her, which was pretty much all the time, and hope to win her over in time.

Or the third option, to suspend the contract, return home for a while, let both her and his crazy thoughts simmer on a low back burner for a while, and then maybe return to Gull Island later. Once they both had time to clearly think things through.

Flipping over again, giving the pillow another thump, he wondered what was option number four.

———

Raven went downstairs for a cup of tea and some toast. She was in the mood for something light. Spotting a couple of Sebastian's camera cases, where he had left them stashed along the hall, she picked them up. Since there was no telling when he would return for his equipment, she ought to just keep everything in his room for now. She set them along the wall with the others. He certainly had a lot of equipment.

Moving to the closet, which was left partially open, she started to push the door shut, only to pause and look inside. Four worn jeans and three flannel shirts hung neatly on the pole. An extra pair of boots sat under the jeans. The twin duffel bags, folded neatly, rested on the shelf.

In the bathroom was his shaving kit, where the scent of his woodsy aftershave hung the heaviest, alongside a bottle of green apple shampoo and a stick of some musky deodorant.

Feeling just a tiny bit guilty, but not enough to stop, she opened the dresser drawers. Nothing in the bottom. The middle held an assortment of shirts. The top drawer held socks and underwear. Resting on the antique lace doily was a worn black book. She had seen this little notebook before. That night he played his sax on the gazebo.

Feeling a chill, she picked up the notebook and a stubby pencil that fell from the inside and took both to the bed. Opening to the first page, she read his neat cursive handwriting.

Running her fingertips over the words on the pages, she read sentence fragments, rhyming words, many crossed out and replaced with new ones, lines of melodies. Some had dates added or notes of reference. Many did not. Some were complete paragraphs, or stanzas, she supposed they might be called, some were only fragmented thoughts.

A poet's soul. It hit her like a hammer's blow. Sebastian had a poet's soul. The words were beautiful, and she knew from first-hand experience that the music was hauntingly beautiful or perhaps upbeat and cheery. To judge from the words, he could do both.

Turning more pages, she halted when she had reached the end of his musings so far. Dated the night she watched him; her breath hitched as she read the words he had penned as she had watched.

He penned words of mystery, of love. He spoke of dreams and treasure. He wrote of her. Her name stared back at her. Gasping, she realized he had started a love song about her. Or to her. Scribbled-out words, replaced with stronger ones, made her pause, as if it seemed he had been searching his own heart and mind that night, to see what he was experiencing.

Suddenly, feeling like an intruder, she quickly returned the notebook to the dresser and left the room, securing the door behind her. She realized he had already fallen in love with her then. Her heart raced as she made her way outside to the cool air.

No wonder he was willing to transform into a dog to

keep her safe and risk injury when he went after Arthur. Doubtlessly, he had been nearby, watching, as she was up on the widow's walk. Sebastian Knight was in love with her. Going down the stone path, following the sound of rushing waves, she felt goosebumps rising.

———

"Commander Koynes, nice of you to come visit me," Sebastian greeted him the next morning. He'd been told to expect to leave soon, and when he heard boots approaching his room, he hoped it was one of the seamen assigned to take him to the boats. Seeing Raven's brother enter was not one of the things he was expecting.

Commander Koynes stood in the doorway, a bemused smile upon his face. "So, you're the man who's getting under my sister's skin? Interesting."

Sebastian forced down a hard swallow. From what he'd seen and heard, this was no man to be trifled with. "Perhaps you ought to sit down a moment," he suggested, waving to the room's other chair.

"I just wanted a few words with you before you were released, Mr. Knight."

"Absolutely. What about, other than your sister, of course?"

"About pressing charges of your own against the May siblings and Dudley Jones."

They discussed the Coast Guard's stance against their property, specifically Gull Island and its light station, as well as further charges against one of its legal tenants, Raven. As a contracted visitor, Sebastian could also be added for harm done to him.

"Let me think about it, okay, Commander. It sounds

like you already have a strong enough case against them, considering the things they did to me. Truthfully, my issues are pretty mild compared to what they put Raven through."

Koynes nodded. "Except you're the one sporting that," he said, nodding to his snowy arm brace. "What was the final count? One hundred and thirty-eight stitches?"

"Something like that. I'll probably be more inclined to count them when they come out, I guess. Still, I witnessed the way it affected Raven. To me, that counts worse than trying to drive a shovel through someone's arm."

Koynes considered that. "Spoken like a man with feelings for someone else. Strong feelings. We could add cruelty to animals," Koynes added. "If we could find the dog. Rave said he disappeared into the island's interior."

"He might have crawled off to try nursing his own wound," Sebastian suggested vaguely. Surely Raven had not said anything later to her brother? The man seemed to accept his suggestion easily enough. "Can I ask you something, Commander?"

Koynes nodded, leaning forward in his chair.

"Doesn't it bother you that she's out there all alone? That she's been out there like that for five years?"

Koynes smiled, leaning back. "Of course it does," he said. "But hopefully you spent enough time around Rave to notice she has her own ideas about things."

Sebastian nodded, smiling at the phrase. Did she ever.

Koynes tipped forward once more, hands resting on his knees. "Raven is like a rose. She's beautiful, but she's wild. She's fragile, but she's tough. She needs tender handling, but she can survive just about anything."

Sebastian again smiled, liking the comparison. Had he not thought himself that she was like a rose?

Koynes let out a breath. "I've gotten to the point, years

ago, where I don't want to get stuck by her thorns anymore. So, I've learned to just back off when she's thorny. It hurts less that way."

Ah, but sometimes it was fun to play among those thorns, just to see what happened. "She showed me her paintings. She told me about why she was out there. How long can she continue to live like that?"

"As long as she wants. I made sure her lease has no expiration date unless she wishes to terminate it. She has a steady source of income." He spread out his hands. "So to answer your question, Mr. Knight, indefinitely."

What was another five years out there? Or ten more after that? A lifetime?

Koynes paused, searching around the room. He finally settled his gaze back to Sebastian. "After we lost our parents, Rave felt it was her responsibility to look after the younger two kids. Robin and Lark. Especially Lark, as he was barely more than a baby back then. Raven pretty much raised those two by herself." He stopped, dusting off his pant legs. "She has learned to be strong, resourceful, and resilient. But I remember another Raven. The girl before our parents died. She was a delightful imp." Stopping again, he smiled at the memories, rubbing his hands together.

Sebastian felt himself moving forward in his chair, captivated by the story and the twinkle in the man's eye. Thinking of her graduation photo, he wished he could picture Raven as a young impish girl.

"She had the prettiest smile and the quickest laugh," Commander Koynes continued. "She loved to play games. Any kind of games. She just loved everything and anything. She gave her whole heart to life. She was pure and innocent." He stopped again, his dreamy expression altering. He coughed once. "It was a shame she had to lose all that."

Speechlessly, Sebastian took in the man's words, knowing there was a reason he was sharing such personal information. It whet his appetite to learn more about the thorny Miss Raven Koynes. But should he be telling her brother that?

"One more thing, Mr. Knight, here," Koynes said, reaching for a black garment he had carried into the room. "A coat for the trip over. Since you were transported to the mainland without a chance to collect a coat."

Surprised, he blinked, accepting the coat, looking at the official Coast Guard insignia.

"Well, this is really nice of you, Commander. I appreciate it."

Koynes shrugged, rising to his feet. "You still have that contract with the island light station. You would freeze to death on the ride over in just that T-shirt," he said, a ghost of a smile on his lips. "Besides, you can always give it back to me later."

"I promise I'll get it back to you soon. Thanks."

Koynes waved him off. "When you are ready, I have two seamen posted downstairs to take you to the boat."

"I'm ready." Still not sure of which option he was going with, he did know he was ready to get back to Raven and all her delightful, mysterious thorns. At least he had a few more pieces of the puzzle.

———

Raven jumped, startled by the boat's horn. Her paintbrush trailed across the canvas, and she hastily plunked it into the jar of cleaner and raced to the window. Her heart beat as she made out the Coast Guard boat easing alongside the dock. Was it Wren returning? Or Sebastian?

Hastily, she pulled off her paint smock and glasses before dashing down the stairs. Grabbing her jacket and scarf from the peg at the door, she went outside to meet the boat.

Sebastian stood on the dock, dressed in her brother's coat. A seaman joined him, carrying several wooden crates over and lining them up.

"Hi. Uh, Wren sent groceries," Sebastian said, indicating the crates. He reached for one more from the seaman aboard the boat. "Wren said it's to replace anything that might have spoiled during the outage."

"That was thoughtful of him."

Finished unloading their guest and groceries, the seaman reversed the engines, easing the boat away from the dock, giving Raven a friendly salute. She returned the action, her gaze once more settled on Sebastian.

"So....new coat?" she asked.

"Yeah, on loan from your brother since my leather one is still here."

Yes, guiltily, she had buried her nose in it last night, and even slipped it on, searching for his smell. Searching for comfort.

"I hung it back on the peg by the door," she said slowly, aware of the tension building within her, around them, even in the vast space surrounding them.

Recalling the words Sebastian had penned, describing his thoughts, finding his feelings for her, she felt rooted to the spot. Thinking of how he'd transformed into Salzburg, still unable to reconcile the two as one in her mind, she felt awkward, almost heavy under his green-eyed gaze.

"So, can I come in?" he finally asked.

She blinked as heat reached her cheeks. "Yes." Reaching and grabbing a crate, she carefully avoided the ones closest to him and headed for the house.

He made one more trip out to get crates, and she made two more, quietly reminding him he was injured.

"Tea?" she asked when he returned with the last one.

"Sure."

She put the kettle on to boil, and he shrugged out of the borrowed jacket. Carefully hanging it up, he straddled a chair, waiting for the kettle.

She caught his smile as the Grandfather clock chimed, and the kettle whistled.

"So, you'll be okay?" She nodded at the white bandage and brace on his arm.

"Yeah. They said it could've been much worse."

How much worse would it have been had the injury occurred while he was in human form?

He grinned. "I told them he tossed the shovel, and my arm happened to be in the way."

"Probably a good idea to go with that story," she stated. Sebastian was no doubt used to having to alter things to explain being...shifted. The kettle whistled louder. She removed it from the burner, filled two cups, and added the tea bags to steep.

"It must be nice to have the power back on again?"

"It is." It was even better having him back again. Except she had no clue what to say or do. The urge to keep moving her hands about was almost overpowering.

After a couple of minutes, she pulled the tea bags and set a cup before him, aware he watched her every move. "Milk?"

He shook his head side to side, adding a lump of sugar to his cup and stirring.

She poured milk and two lumps of sugar, joining him at the table. Words formed in her mind, but she couldn't force them out.

Sebastian set the cup aside. "Raven, last night I spent a great deal of time thinking about what to do here."

"Do?"

"Yeah, about the contract for the shoot, and about what you know about me. I know it freaks you out, and I'm sorry. I wish you never had to see any of that, or experience any of the things you did. But I'm also happy that I was on hand to help you through the ordeal, in whatever method I had to use. I am not sorry for that."

He paused, folding his arms over the chair back. "I can't change what happened any more than I can change what I am, what I can do. I can only hope you can accept it as just being a part of me."

Suddenly, she found her voice. "Sebastian, we are not talking about accepting someone with their hairstyle, eye color, or weight. We're talking about the fact you can change yourself into animals at will. That is not a normal, average thing to just ask someone to accept." Her eyes fell on the bracelet. "You said once, if you took that off, the magic would be broken, and you would be left in that form forever." She licked her lips, searching his face. "Have you ever considered it?"

He fingered the leather and circled the stones, and she imagined his fingers touching her like that. Heat fanned through her.

"You mean deliberately taking it off, knowing I'll never be able to shift again?"

"Yes." Her breath caught.

He blew out a breath, running a hand through his hair. "Raven, that is a lot to expect someone to do. To even consider. I see a lot of advantages to my gift. I could tell you fantastic stories of things I have seen and experienced while shifted into other forms. To willingly give that up forever would be a mighty hard thing to do."

"Impossible?"

"Maybe."

"So you've never considered it?" she asked softly.

"No, I guess not."

"I see." Rising to her feet, she walked quietly away, leaving her teacup untouched.

———

Sebastian pushed his cup aside, watching her go. He considered calling her back into the room, or better yet, going after her, but then decided against it. If he pressed her now, she'd come back fighting. When he first heard her footsteps on the wooden planking, he turned, heart in his throat, wondering what sort of reception she had in mind. As she slowed her approach, he caught the smell of paint thinner wafting from her and knew where she had come from. Had it been a form of therapy, or merely to pass the time, and attempts to return to normal?

He tried to picture her with those big black glasses perched on her face, and he'd bet they slid halfway down her nose. Lost in concentration, she'd be adorable. And sexy hot.

Yet her reception was cool, so he focused on getting the crates of provisions in without damaging his arm. All things considered, it was going better than he had hoped for. She hadn't pushed him into the water.

Waiting for their tea, the Grandfather clock in the other room chimed deeply, and he smiled to himself. Here, on Raven's island, time seemed to stand still. The pine burned invitingly in the fireplace in the next room, wafting into the kitchen. She smelled great, so he would bet she had bathed recently. Rich floral scents teased him as she moved about with her efficient grace.

137

Well, he was back, she was mad, and he was clueless about what to do about the whole thing. Removing the bracelet was beyond unthinkable. How could he ever get her to see a positive side to his ability? Absently, he toyed with it until a flash of white caught his eye.

"Well, Madeline, at least *you* haven't deserted me. If you want some tea, there's an extra cup."

CHAPTER
NINE

Sebastian walked into the living room. Raven sat on the sofa, holding an old book almost in tatters. He stopped, waiting until she met his gaze.

"Can we talk?" he asked softly.

She got up, shelved the book, and went to the fire. She added a log and poked the older ones, sending sparks flying up the chimney and heat out into the room.

"All done with your pictures?"

Her tone bit with sarcasm. And pain. And fear. He wished he could ease her concerns.

"For now. Can we have a moment, please?"

"I believe we already did. Nothing seems to have changed."

Sebastian blew out a long breath. She was not going to make things easy on him. He took another step toward her. Her shoulders tensed. Her wary stare nearly undid him. He'd never felt so torn in different directions. What he loved to do was the one thing she despised.

He squeezed his eyes shut for a moment. Seeking...

The pressure started pounding behind his eyeballs. Still, she awaited with her arms folded. And he wanted to kiss that indifferent stare off her face. Touch her porcelain skin with his thumbs. He swallowed.

"Raven? I don't know what to do. Will you please talk to me?" He held his hands out to her.

She gave him a full body stare down, and her eyes narrowed. "Are you still going to take those pictures?"

He'd never doubted his work before. Until now. "I have too. It's my job." He shook his head, feeling his shoulders slump. "Can you talk to me?"

"Frankly, I don't see the point."

———

Brushing past him, she exited the room, stealing all the warmth with her.

She was doing her best to avoid him, Sebastian decided, following her to the kitchen. She stood at the window, looking out. Her face gave none of her thoughts away, but her body language sure did.

He swallowed back a groan of disappointment when she stiffly walked to the fire and coaxed it to life. Except it was already burning briskly, as flames eagerly licked the recently added fuel. A low sigh escaped him. He'd spent most of the day outside, giving her time, giving himself distractions. Now it was late, and he knew they couldn't avoid each other forever if he stayed long enough to accomplish anything on his to-do list. What was he supposed to do about her?

Without a word, she grabbed her coat, scarf, and gloves and, once dressed, walked out the back door.

Sinking into a chair, burying his head in his hands, he could almost cry, not having the faintest clue how to deal with her.

———

Wrapping her arms around herself to ward off the cold despite her coat, gloves, and scarf, she stepped further out onto the narrow outcropping, stepping lightly to the very edge. She stopped when the toes of her boots touched the spot where the waves lapped the rocks. Standing straight and tall, like the gnarled tree behind her, she drew in deep, heavy breaths of cold, crisp air, tinged with mingled lake scents of fish.

The sun was setting over the endless miles of water, with vivid yellows and vibrant golds dressing the lake in breathtaking robes of color. It was, Raven mused, what Sebastian would call a painted sky. Darn, she went and did it again. How had he become such a driving part of her thoughts and life in such a short time? It wasn't fair, even when she was mad at him, he could occupy so many of her thoughts.

Sweeping the vast lake expanse, she searched for answers where the sky met the lake. Breathtaking, but silent. She wished her heart were half as quiet. Shivering from the cold, she waited for the growing darkness, wishing she knew what to do.

———

Sebastian decided he was being lousy and followed her outside when she clearly wanted to be left alone. But darn it, he couldn't stay away forever. It had killed him all day to leave her be, to go prowling around the island taking pictures of things that now held little interest. With dusk approaching, and her outside with the dropping temperatures, he would be nearby, and she would have to stick out her thorns if she didn't like him being present.

He pulled on a coat and picked up one of the cameras. Slinging the strap over his shoulder out of habit, he doubted he'd actually use it. Wrapping the scarf around his neck, he stepped off the porch and went in search of Raven. More than likely, she didn't go too far.

He stopped dead in his tracks. His heart slammed against his ribs. She stood on a narrow chunk of rock that extended far into the lake, surrounded by the sunset and the wind. A long, gnarled pine tree stood behind her, the tip leaning close to the water, bent and bare from years of rough winter lake exposure. The sparse green boughs framed her perfectly. The lake, brilliantly aglow with late sunset colors, set the best backdrop, silhouetting her. Dark blue water splashed near her feet and stretched out and away in shades of blue and grey.

She was lovely with the wind tossing her dark hair like the mane of a wild mare. The mental image fit her well. Unable to resist the sight, he snatched the camera and snapped several shots. He was, after all, a nature photographer. She was as untamed and natural as the island around her.

"Yeah, right," he muttered into the wind. Nature be hanged, he was capturing Raven's wild splendor, her angry beauty, and he knew it.

Photos taken, he set the camera down. Twilight chased the sunset splendor away. Stars came out, twinkling over the lake, and moonlight shone through the patchy clouds. Waves lapped the rocks, breaking the uneasy silence. Would she poke him again with her thorns if he joined her on the rocky shore? Or would she push him into the water? He wouldn't put it past her. No doubt, Raven was capable of just about anything.

Glancing around, a wisp of white caught his eye. Off by the house, just off the porch, stood Madeline, watching them. Hands hanging at her sides, the girl hovered a few inches above the ground, wind blowing her dress.

Okay, what did the ghost want him to do? Like before, Madeline simply waited, her face showing no expression. How could you possibly know what a ghost was thinking?

Madeline was going to have to deal with it. He was more interested in Raven.

He wrapped his arms around her waist, and she stiffened.

"Quite the view you have here," he said in a low voice, his breath warm against her cold neck.

The repetition of the waves slapping the rocks was almost lulling.

"This is relaxing," he said. If it weren't for the bitter cold wind blowing on them.

"It can be."

A palatable silence hung between them. She seemed impervious to the chill that sent a shiver throughout his body. He wasn't sure what was bothering him more, her silence or the wind.

"Are you hungry?" he asked, receiving only silence for his question. *That's right.* She seemed to resent his questions. He tried again, rephrasing the question as a comment, "I made dinner. It's not much, but it's hot and ready."

Nothing.

"I was kind of hoping you would join me."

Still nothing, but there was a slight drop in the tension as her rigid body relaxed. Taking heart, he plowed onward.

"You don't have to talk to me. You can just sit there and eat."

No words.

"I won't ask any questions, and I'll even clean up afterward."

She sagged a little against him. Telling himself it was her giving in, not just fatigue from standing so long. He smiled, reached for her hand, and turned her around. Remembering what she had told Salzburg about his disarming smile, he kept his expression neutral. Out of respect for her, he didn't want to use the information he'd gained while in dog form.

"It would mean a lot to me if you came and joined me." He would ensure that every phrase he said was worded as a positive statement, with no questions. Even if it killed him.

Wordlessly, Raven nodded, edging off the rocky outcropping. Holding his hand, she let him lead her into the house.

From the corner of his eye, he spotted Madeline as she slowly faded away.

———

Raven had sensed Sebastian's approach before she heard his boots on the rocks. Squeezing her eyes shut, she waited, breath held. Thankfully, the winds had mercy on her and stole his rugged scent before being tempted to do something like jump into his arms. She allowed herself to smile at his discomfort with silence. For a man who had a largely solitary career, how did he stand the stillness and quiet of nature?

Relenting, she trailed him to the house, wondering how he cooked.

As soon as she entered the house, rich, heavy scents greeted her as she removed her outer gear, hanging it alongside his. Something about the action seemed so right. Comforting. Coming in from the cold together, undressing and hanging up their coats side by side, about to meet for dinner.

Closing her ears to the whispering in her mind, she marched off to clean up. Joining him a few minutes later at the dining room table, he had set two places, three sittings away from each other. A way to respect her desire for distance, no doubt. He placed two big bowls in the middle and sat down, wordlessly watching her.

A basket of steaming rolls sat on the table, as did a bottle of wine and two wineglasses. Wine? Oh yes, left over from when Wren, Robin, Ricky, and Lark had come for New Year's two years ago. Hopefully, it aged well.

"I hope you don't mind me getting the wine out," he said as she sat. "To judge by the dust on the bottle, you hadn't used it in a while. So I figured it was fair game. Tonight's offering is nothing fancy, just some stuff I found around the pantry. Pasta and sauce. Maybe a few herbs crushed in for good measure." Taking a twirl with his fork, he held up the bite. "Anyway, enjoy."

She did. It was delicious. He could cook, making something as ordinary as pasta and canned sauce taste like something from a gourmet restaurant. It was the herbs, but she could never get the blends to taste quite like this. And the rolls were buttery soft. The wine added just the final touch. The only thing missing was candlelight. Too bad the power wasn't still out. It would afford the perfect excuse to require candlelight. She suspected he would use that excuse if he thought he could.

It took effort, but she remained silent through dinner, avoiding making eye contact for the most part. He quickly gave up any attempts at conversation. At least the tension seemed to have eased a little between them. Finished, she headed for the living room while he made good on his deal to clean up.

By the time he had finished, she had escaped to her painting room, with the door closed. Inside the safety and relaxing atmosphere, she readjusted her glasses and studied the painting on the easel. Another view of the tower, shrouded in fluffy clouds and wheeling gulls, was not shaping up like she envisioned. Maybe it was the wine. Or dinner. Or the company.

She missed having Salzburg to talk to. Already, in such a short time, the dog, or Sebastian as the dog, had made her aware of her need to talk out her feelings to another. And, *oh boy*, did she have some feelings to talk out.

Maybe she could call Robin tomorrow and bend her ear a little. But Robin had so much to deal with already. This was her first pregnancy, and the doctors said she risked complications if she didn't take it easy. Ricky would be furious with her if she somehow upset Robin over this thing with Sebastian.

Setting her brush aside, she considered any other options. Lark? No, he was too busy with college over on the mainland. And far too young and inexperienced with matters of the heart. Wren? Well, she had a feeling she knew where her closest sibling's allegiance fell. Wren could have given Sebastian any Guard coat. But he gave him one of his personal coats. Sebastian may or may not realize the significance of that, but she sure did. And since coming to Gull Island, she had lost touch with any remaining friends from her former life. Who did that leave?

No one. The same no one she had talked to for the last five years. Unless you count Madeline. It took some time, but she couldn't help but open up to the ghost, who seemed content enough to listen for a while before silently fading away. She wished the girl would show up right now.

"Madeline?" she whispered.

Nothing. No wispy form appeared. She shrugged. Sometimes it worked, and sometimes it did not. Oh well, worth a try at least.

Dipping her brush in the jar of cleaner, she removed her glasses, giving up on the project for now. She crept slowly downstairs and pulled on her winter gear. She walked over the grounds with her arms wrapped around her sides to ward off the windy chill.

Stopping by the tower, she looked around. "Madeline?" she called again. Tonight, it was worthy of a second try.

———

Sebastian leaned against the wall by the window seat with heavy eyes. Something white flashed by the glass, startling and perking him up. Following the blur, he pressed his hands and face to the cold pane, looking down, amazement stealing over him.

Raven and Madeline were standing outside by the tower, and he could swear they were talking. Or at least Raven was talking, and the ghost was listening.

Amazed, he knelt there, watching the scene. She would talk to a dog and a teenage girl dead for how many centuries, but she wouldn't talk to him? Unbelievable. A mysterious rose did not begin to describe Raven Koynes.

"You have got to be kidding," he muttered, checking the time on the clock on his dresser. It was almost midnight. Did she frequently go out in the middle of the night to talk to dead people? Somehow, he doubted it. He also doubted she was talking about anything but him.

For one crazy second, he considered shifting, becoming a proverbial fly on the wall. Or tower in this case. He almost wished he could become Salzburg again. Then, thinking better of it, he looked closer.

He could not hear the conversation, though it looked mostly one-sided, but he could see her expressions. The worry lines around her eyes and lips eased. The heaviness she had worn so recently gradually fell away. Whatever else she discussed with Madeline, it helped her. Whatever his thoughts or misgivings about Madeline, right now, he was glad she was around for Raven.

———

"Raven?" Sebastian's voice called, as she reached the bottom step the next morning.

"How do you like your eggs?"

Eggs? Following his voice, she entered the kitchen to find him standing at the stove, fry pan in one hand, spatula awkwardly held in another, and a dozen eggs on the counter. His thick wool socks made no noise as he slid across the floor. His smile tripped the beating of her heart. The smell of brewing coffee drew her to the pot.

"Scrambled," she replied, reaching for a cup.

His smile was huge. "What a coincidence. Scrambled is the only way I can make them," he replied, turning back to the stove.

She didn't believe that for a second. Any man who could make ordinary pasta and sauce as good as he had last night should be able to make something as simple as eggs stand up and dance.

For whatever reason, her chat last night with Madeline helped ease some of the anxiety in her heart. Somehow, after explaining the shifting issues that plagued her, she felt more able to talk to Sebastian again. If not about his ability, at least as the man she knew was in love with her. And one she was slowly trusting with her heart.

"Good," she commented a few minutes later, between bites of scrambled eggs and toast loaded with boysenberry jam.

"Thanks. So where did the jam come from? It's different."

She bit back the grin tugging at her lips. Shifting into

animals and asking endless questions. Both seemed to be an ingrained part of him. "A friend of Wren's from the mainland. His name is Ezra. They grow wild about his place. Everyone knows Ezra makes the best boysenberry jam around."

"That wouldn't be the same Ezra from the boat shop that rented me that pitiful little boat my first trip out here, would it?" Sebastian asked between bites.

"The same. I am sort of surprised he gave you such a tiny boat, or any boat at all, knowing the storm was coming along."

"I suspect he was trying to drown me."

She shook her head, reaching for another piece of toast. Apparently, that would have been a waste of effort. "I doubt it. Probably trying to warn you." More than likely, if someone wanted to drown him, he'd just change into a fish.

"Warn me? Of what?"

"Ezra is one of the few who know why I'm out here. Being Wren's friend, it's hard to say what all he knows," she said with a shrug. "Anyway, he can be a little overprotective of me as well. Doubtlessly, he was suspicious when you asked for a boat to Gull Island."

When the food was gone, the plates empty, and the coffee carafe half drunk, she scooted her chair back, rising. "Well, Mr. Knight, another good meal. I'll clean up this time." She reached for his plate, their fingers touching as he handed it over.

Heat sizzled, and she was sure she saw sparks jump. Not even the fires in the fireplace sparked like that.

Drawing back, the plates slipped, and she managed to regain control before they fell to the floor. Staring at him, her lips parted. In anticipation? She forced herself to lick them closed.

He coughed once. "Well, I'll be outside. I need to get..."

He let the words trail, pulling himself away from the kitchen toward the door.

Heart beating rapidly, she watched him go, then moved to the sink and washed the dishes, barely aware of the soapy water. She'd enjoyed their brief conversation entirely too much. She enjoyed their time together too much. Like when they came in last night and hung up their coats next to each other. It just felt right. She could become too accustomed to this.

Except he was a shapeshifter.

But he also had a touch that ignited something new within her. Those sparks startled her. But they excited her too. Thrilled her. Looking into those green eyes of his, she was sorely tempted to drop the dishes and fly into his arms, holding him tight.

But what would he have done if she had? She dared not ask. She wasn't sure she could stop herself once she asked him to start something. She certainly couldn't be sure where he would take it.

No wonder Helen had been so besotted with him, she mused, pulling the plug. Except Helen didn't know what Raven did. Moving to the window, she glanced out, finding him at the tower, standing on the widow's walk. Yes, she understood what he was doing up there. Feeling the wind on your face, with only the gulls and clouds for company, it was the very best place to sort out heavy thoughts. Then her gaze fell on the coat he'd left behind.

———

Sebastian grimaced, wishing he'd put on a jacket. Dummy. It took everything he'd had inside him to drag his eyes off those lips of hers once she licked them. They were going to be the death of him yet. They might be worth all the thorns he would have to endure for one kiss. And the curiousness in her eyes as he forced himself to leave caught him more than a little off-guard. And, in his mind-muddled state, he'd gone and left his outerwear inside.

Minutes later, he realized he'd climbed the light tower. He'd unconsciously brought a camera case along but not a jacket.

He shook his head, sure he was losing his mind because of her. And, as if to convince himself he was right, the swirling wind carried a tease of her perfume. He closed his eyes, inhaling deeply.

"Here, I thought you might want this," Raven said softly.

Turning suddenly with his hand against his chest, she held his jacket out for him as if it were a peace offering.

"It gets chilly up here," she offered by way of explanation as he accepted the garment and slipped it on.

"Thank you," he said, glad for the sudden warmth. "The view is really something from up here," he said, careful to avoid questions this time.

"I like it. It's good therapy for someone who has important thinking to do."

He chuckled softly, peeking at her. "Is it that obvious that's what I'm doing up here?" So much for no questions. Oh well.

She nodded, a tiny grin about to betray her and captivate his attention.

"Darn, I was hoping you would just think I was taking some dynamite pictures."

She shook her head, nodding to the camera case he had left discarded inside the glasshouse. "Not with that still in there."

Oh. He shrugged, giving her a sheepish grin.

"So, what were you so deep in thought about?" she asked.

He lifted a brow. *She* was in the mood to ask questions? He considered her question, staring at the lake's choppy surface. "Lots of things, actually. But more directly, I suppose it is the beauty of Gull Island. I came here with the intention of capturing the beauty, life, and spirit of it. Capture it on film, I mean and instead look at what has happened." He slid a sideways glance at her, holding her gaze for a moment before continuing.

"Despite everything, I can't seem to find all of that. As a photographer, I know it's here." He gave a laugh. "Kind of like Arthur and his insane quest for treasure, I guess. I know Gull Island's heart and spirit are here somewhere. I can feel it, sense it, smell it, and breathe it." He touched his chest. Perhaps he was inhaling and savoring her scent. "I just can't find all the components of the island enough to photograph and capture it."

He blew out a breath, stuffing his hands in the pockets of the jacket, leaning away from the railing. "It's like the painted skies. They're real. You saw them last night. I can see them, I can smell them, feel them, almost taste them. But whatever I put on film is never honest enough about them."

He stomped his foot once on the widow's walk stone, casting her another sideways look. "I bet that sounds pretty silly to someone else, but it's what I was thinking about. Well, one thing I was thinking about."

"I don't think it's particularly silly looking at it from a photographer's view. Probably like looking for an answer to a problem that should be obvious but isn't. Wish I could help you in finding what you're looking for, but I wouldn't know it if I tripped over it." She drew in an uneven breath. "So, what else has your mind buzzing?"

"Us." His answer was immediate and without thought. "How sorry I am about how things went earlier and how I feel about you, and how shocked you must be about it. And not being able to undo or change anything. It's just plain frustrating."

"Shocked? Yes, that is one word." She turned to him. "You have to admit learning what you can do, seeing what you can do, is a bit of a shock."

He nodded.

"And," she drew in a long, slow breath. "And to have you deceive me by pretending to be a stray dog. I know you had noble purposes in mind, but you still took advantage of the situation, and it makes it hard to trust someone like that. You must admit this is not your normal sort of situation. For us."

His heart skipped a beat at the way she said 'us'. "Well, now that I've had time to think it over, I really wish I had told you that next morning who Salzburg really was. I could've been honest with you, and we still could've used the situation to keep Arthur in line." He searched her eyes where tears glistened. He gently placed his thumbs to collect the warm moisture. Shattered. He was shattered. The liquid warmth oozed through the cracks of his soul and pierced his heart.

"Raven, I am sorry." His voice cracked. "Forgive me?"

Her hands gripped the railing as she faced the water. The wind was coming from the west, sweeping across the vast expanse of the lake, bringing heavy scents on its currents. She didn't appear to notice the view. She nodded once. "Yes. That sounds like it would've been the best plan, now that it's too late." She turned back to him again. "But if you'd told me the truth the next day, I'm not sure I would've even believed you. How could anyone believe such a tale, Sebastian? Even witnessing it, I still have trouble believing you're a shapeshifter."

She hiccupped, holding back the tears. His heart melted like paper on fire.

"Raven, please don't," he pleaded, rubbing his thumbs under her eyes, tilting her chin up.

Blinking, she pulled free with another hiccup. She waved into the wild wind. "Do you ever think about just flying away? Like the birds?"

Shifting into anything was the furthest thing from his mind. "Not right now."

She gave him a tight smile. "I can't seem to figure out how I should feel."

Hauling her into his arms, he said, "Raven, honey, you have to follow your heart. That's all you can do."

"That's the problem."

He smiled, understanding. Understanding all too well, unfortunately. "I know it's hard," he said softly. "You must be feeling a whole lot of stuff lately."

She nodded, and his breath hitched as an idea struck him. Once more searching her eyes, damp despite her best efforts, he smiled, rubbing his thumb along her cheeks.

"Would you like to come with me when I leave?" he asked brightly. "Come home with me once I am done here? Get off the island for just a little while?"

CHAPTER
TEN

"Home?" Raven asked Sebastian.

"Yes." He nodded. "Well, to where I call home between assignments. We can work through things without the memories so recent of what happened here." He sucked in a breath. "Consider it a fresh start?"

She looked into those eyes, her heart taking flight. The idea appealed to her. Hadn't Wren suggested more or less the same thing? But something held her back. Turning to the lake, stretching out before her in never-ending shades of blues and greens, she searched for the answers.

She'd been experiencing more emotions in the last few days than she had in years. And feeling more alive than before. *That's* why she wanted to fly like the birds. To have a way to vent what churned within her. She didn't fully understand this new sense of freedom that came when Sebastian untied the last few knots in her heart. But how could she get him to understand that? Especially when she did not fully understand herself. Or the resulting fear of the unknown that plagued her. And the fear of his known shifting abilities. Between the incredible high of the freedom and the incredible doubts and fears. It made her dizzy.

"Let me think about it, Sebastian," she said. "When do you think you'll be ready to leave?"

He shrugged. "I don't know. A few more days yet." He smiled, cradling her face in his hands. "Plenty of time for you to mull it over."

Resting against his hands and leaning into his strength, she closed her eyes with the wind swirling around them. She could die happy right now. Is that what real love feels like?

"Look, how about you come and take some pictures with me?"

"Me? I know nothing about photography. Especially at the level you do."

"So?" He discounted her hasty denial with a wag of his head. "I am not asking you to join me as a fellow photographer."

She tilted her head to one side. "What would be the purpose of my coming along then?" She anxiously licked her lips, waiting for his answer.

"I would enjoy your company," he replied gruffly, capturing her lips in a satisfying kiss.

Wide-eyed, she released a surprised whimper while slowly relaxing into his strength. A warmth spread throughout her body. She melted against him, fitting so well, liking how they molded together like twin spoons. Her fingers worked under the layers of his shirts, pulling them free from his pants, till her fingertips touched his heated skin.

She liked how he kissed, strong and gentle at the same time. Giving but also taking. As her fingers roved the muscles of his abdomen and back, he groaned, holding her tight, making her feel safe and dizzy at the same time.

Like most things he did, Sebastian was a good kisser.

What else would he be good at?

"You have no idea how long I waited for that," he said, finally breaking the spell between them. "It was worth every second."

Breathless and a little stunned, she managed a shaky smile, gripping the rail to steady her reeling senses. "I'm glad you weren't disappointed with having to wait so long for it." She regarded him for a moment. "So why didn't you just kiss me like that when you first wanted to?"

"Why don't you show me your favorite places, Raven?" he asked, quickly changing the subject instead. He took her hand and led her inside the glasshouse. "The places you go to when you want to seek inspiration for your paintings. When you put those big black glasses on your face and create those lovely works of art."

Not releasing her hand, he swung the camera case with his free hand onto his shoulder and led her down the stairs.

"Are you making fun of me?" she demanded.

Chuckling, he shook his head. "Not at all. Retract those thorns of yours. I was merely pointing out how I envision you at work in your studio. Now, show me your secret places."

———

Heaven help him, but he'd been powerless to stop himself this time. Taking a deep breath, he plunged ahead, capturing her lips in a satisfying kiss, before he could talk himself out of it or she could jab a thorn into him. When her fingers pulled his shirts free and explored his boiling hot skin, he thought he might melt on the spot. Or send them both up in flames. He'd only stopped when their lungs screamed for fresh air.

Licking his lips, he tasted her berry lip gloss and smiled.

Oh, but that kiss was worth waiting for. He had expected thorns and would've relished them this time. Instead, she offered her soft petals and eager fingers. Raven Koynes knew how to yield to a man kissing her. Who would have ever thought? Watching her lick her lips again, he considered another kiss.

Before he acted on impulse, he stepped aside for her to lead him.

She guided him to the rocky outcropping where she had stood last night. In the light of day, with a faint fog swirling around, he snapped photos as she hugged the old pine tree, the wind blowing her hair.

Next, she took him toward the woods and hills leading to the island's interior. Among the moss and snow-covered rocks, he found late-season wildflowers cloaked in their summer colors. He excitedly jumped from one rock to another, snapping pictures of the blue, yellow, and white petals. The quaking aspens drew him to a small meadow where she mentioned she sometimes took a nap.

Sebastian grabbed pictures of the perfect fall colors, so famous to the area, as they climbed higher.

"Here. This is why I come up here," she declared, dropping to a rock and dusting away the snow.

Turning, he followed her pointed finger, his breath leaving him in a hiss. Startled, he gazed around. Amazing.

He had not paid attention or realized how high they had climbed, and now the house and tower below were small in comparison. The lake sparkled beneath the clear blue sky. Away from the biting winds and slapping waves, the picture was tranquil and almost ethereal.

Putting the camera's viewfinder to his eye, he pressed the shutter release several times, twisting and kneeling to get views from different vantage points.

Raven drew her knees to her chest, watching him at

work. "I'm glad you see what I do when I came up here and appreciate it."

Sebastian turned, satisfied he had captured some great shots from higher ground of the lake, trees, and the light station. Heart slamming, he positioned the camera, squeezed a few more shots of Raven. The body composition of the way she sat on the rock, arms around her knees, and the way her eyes were lowered gave a sense of emotions rolling over her face like clouds.

In a word, she was enchanting. He longed to know what thoughts tumbled through her mind. Would she tell him if he asked? Pictures done, he set the camera aside. He knelt in front of her and captured her hands in his.

"Raven?" he said cautiously.

"Just thinking," she answered quickly, pulling her hands free to push her hair behind her ear. "You had wanted to see my favorite spots. This is one of them."

Okay, so she was going all prickly again. He sucked in a breath, looking around. "Yes, I can see why it would be." It would be incredible, he thought, to have an entire island to wander around and do as you please at any time. He would never run out of things to take pictures of, he decided, since the island had four distinct seasons in which to enjoy. This view would look entirely different in a couple of months and again a few months after that.

He moved over to sit next to her on the rock. He thought about touching her hand, but her energy vibrated with her signature 'hands off' mode. Instead, he swiveled to face her.

"So, what are you thinking about?" he asked.

"Just stuff."

Okay, he got the point. Reaching for her hand, he quickly pulled her to her feet. "Are you ready to head back?"

"Do you ever stop asking questions?"

He laughed. "Not for long."

———

Madeline met them halfway back, her expression one of urgency. Braking to a stop, Sebastian backpaddled at the sight. Raven dropped her arms, silently waiting. She might've found Sebastian's hesitancy humorous if it hadn't been for Madeline's seriousness. Remembering what she read in the journals, she knew the ghost wasn't playing games.

The ghost raised her arm to point in another direction, higher inland from where they came.

Raven turned to Sebastian. "She wants us to go that way."

"You can understand her? What for?"

"I can partially understand her. I don't know, but there's something she wants to show us. Come on." She reached for his hand, and they fell in step behind the girl as she hovered above the snow-covered ground.

Madeline led them higher where the hills grew tall, and the trees were thick. Groups of deer spooked, bounding away with their white tails flashing in alarm. A few hawks screamed overhead. In the distance, a wolf watched them pass from its rocky perch.

"Do you have any idea where she's taking us?" Sebastian whispered, breaking the silence.

Raven shook her head. "She can hear you, so whispering isn't necessary. But we're almost on the other side now. Can you smell the water again?" This was further than she had ever traveled before in her explorations.

Madeline drew to a stop next to a tall rocky formation. She turned to them.

"Now what?" Sebastian whispered. Madeline favored

him with a look even he could interpret. "Unnecessary to whisper. Sorry. I got it." He turned to Raven.

"I have no idea."

Sebastian moved to the edge of the rock wall when she turned to communicate with Madeline.

"Sebastian!" Raven spun at his startled yelp.

"I'm okay. I was falling backward. Look, this is a cave."

She pulled some of the pine and spruce boughs aside, peering into the dark depths. "Well, I'll be. A natural cave in the hillside."

"You didn't know this was here?"

She fished a penlight from her pocket and waved it around. "No, of course not. I've known that caves were formed on lots of these islands. Water erosion, limestone, and all that. This side of the island is hillier than my side."

Sebastian reached for her light. "Allow me." He pushed more branches out of the way and stepped into the darkness. "It's not really as deep as I had thought," he called over his shoulder. "And I'm pretty sure I can see the back of it."

She followed, resting her hand on his shoulder. The air was still. The space was quiet. She glanced down, checking for bear tracks. Hopefully, this wasn't their hibernating lair.

"Oh my word," Sebastian said, coming to a halt and delivering a low whistle. "I think I know what Madeleine wanted us to see." He shone the light's faint beam over wooden crates. Large wooden crates. Stamped on the edge were the words "Elite Arts and Fine Collectibles. Wisconsin."

They turned to each other, their mouths agape, mirrored expressions on their faces. Raven found her voice first.

"The *Endeavor's* missing cargo. It was here the whole time."

Sebastian ran his hands over the crates. "They're still

intact. Nothing appears damaged. So how did Madeline know they were here? And where is Madeline?"

Turning, Raven saw the ghost was indeed gone. Her task apparently complete, she no doubt returned to wherever it was she had faded away. "I have no idea. She's never mentioned it to me."

Sebastian turned to Raven, a broad smile on his face. "Seems crazy that old Arthur was right after all. Here's his treasure."

She drummed her fingers along the rocky wall. "Yes, but the insurance paid it off. Someone really was stashing it here. I need to let Wren know. The Coast Guard needs to take ownership, at least temporarily. And it needs to be returned to the rightful owners."

"One more question, does Wren know about Madeline?"

"Yes, why?"

He cracked a huge, crooked smile. "Who else would believe a ghost just led us to a cached treasure?"

———

Wren arrived two hours later, with both Coast Guard and police officers. He apologized for the lengthy delay but explained that it took some time to gather the necessary manpower for what she had implied during her phone call.

"I can't believe this stuff was here the whole time," Raven stated again.

"My guess is one of the boats must've recovered the belongings early on and brought it ashore from this side of the island," Wren surmised as he studied the cave's lofty location. "You wouldn't have noticed from your side. And since the boats come from all directions, one heading back west wouldn't have aroused your suspicion."

"And Arthur May probably happened to have a connection with them," one of the police officers surmised. "That would explain how he was aware to come looking for the goods. This will call for a further investigation into his background."

"And it explains his insistence that it was here somewhere, despite everything," Raven added.

"Whoever stored it here had the perfect setup." One of the police officers added as the other one snapped photos of the cave and the crates. Finally, they opened the crate, and a collective hush fell over the group packed into the cave.

"Still in pristine condition," another officer said, bending to study the contents carefully. "It looks like the full manifest is here, Commander."

Wren took Raven by the shoulders. "Thursday is the anniversary of the *Endeavor's* wreck. I suspect whoever stashed the cargo will come then, planning to collect it. I don't want you anywhere on this island when they realize it's missing."

Sebastian gripped her by the waist. "Don't worry. I know the perfect place we can go to while you attend to this matter. She'll be perfectly safe."

———

Raven watched her island home and the alabaster light tower grow smaller as Ezra piloted them across the lake to the mainland. Wren had listened to Sebastian's suggestion and contacted Ezra to take them across as soon as they were ready. Upon his arrival, Ezra offered a half-apology to Sebastian about the boat rental incident. Sebastian offered to have his company's insurance put in the claim for the loss on his behalf. It seemed he could make friends with just about anyone, including Ezra.

Unspoken fears tightened her throat. She wrapped her arms around herself, turning her face to the wind to keep the tears away.

"Cold?" Sebastian asked, bending his head to her as he noticed her shiver.

"Yes," she lied, not able to tell him the truth. The last three days with him had been nice and pleasant, but now, chugging along in Ezra's ferry, she felt nothing positive. Quite the opposite.

"Here," he wrapped his arm around her, pulling her close to him on the seat.

With a final look at her shrinking home, she pushed her nose into his shoulder, inhaling his clean male scent, and closed her eyes.

The art and coins were gone, ferried away after they were discovered days ago. The police and others returned, setting up surveillance and traps, ready if someone returned to the cave. Raven was almost glad to escape, unnerved at the number of people running around her island home.

"You're doing fine, darling," he whispered over the top of her head, pulling her hands into his.

Like fresh honey, the endearment instantly warmed her, going straight to her heart. She twisted her head around to see him clearly. *Darling?* That sounded so...sweet. And intimate.

"It must be hard for you to leave now," he said softly. "But I am so glad you agreed to come. It means a lot to me. You can trust me on this. I will take good care of you out in the world."

Not that she had much choice now, thanks to Madeline and Wren. But she believed him. Heaven help her, she believed him.

Sebastian noticed the sadness flickering in her eyes, and the expression sent a knife plunging to his heart. *She seems so vulnerable right now.* He had to handle her carefully or she might break. He recalled her brother's comment about likening her to a rose. Yes, right now it was time to pull on the gloves and gently prune, to take away her sadness and worry. Without asking questions.

Wren hadn't given her much choice in leaving the island, so he wasn't exactly sure how much was her brother's insistence and how much was at his request. In the end, he supposed it didn't really matter.

They arrived on the mainland and stopped at the Coast Guard station, looking for Wren.

"Just wanted to return your coat, Commander," Sebastian stated, handing it over. "Thanks for the loan."

"Will you be around to testify at the trial of the three invaders?" Wren asked, moving papers out of the way, indicating for them to sit. "They are digging up a lot of background on Arthur May."

Sebastian shrugged. "I'm not sure. I move around a lot." He cut a look over at Raven, as she roamed about the office, shifting pictures and items around, and ignoring Wren's tolerant frown at her. He bit back a smile. "When do you think it will be held?"

"Pretrial will probably be the middle of next month. Before Thanksgiving is the plan. Your willingness to press charges and return to testify will go a long way toward keeping those three from ever going back to Gull Island. Or any other Guard station or shipwreck."

And his sister, Sebastian surmised, liking that idea best of all.

"I will press charges, now that I've thought about it, Commander, and I will do my best to be here for the trial."

"Great. We'll keep you updated as things get scheduled.

So, you two are off to Connecticut now?" he asked, sending Raven another glance.

"Yes, my parents live there, and it's my home between assignments. We have a two o'clock flight."

Wren stood. "In that case, Raven, how about a hug for your big brother? If only to get you to stop rearranging my office."

She stepped into his open arms and gave him a peck on the cheek. "I'll miss you."

"Let me know the minute you return, Rave," he ordered.

Sebastian enjoyed the exchanges between the two siblings. There was a deep love for one another beneath the friendly taunts. It could make him wish he had a sibling. Younger, preferred. After shaking hands, Wren escorted them to the front office. "Seaman, arrange a driver to take these two to the airport."

A man gave Wren a snappy salute and spun, wheeling off to make arrangements. Sebastian marveled at the respect the sailors showed Wren, and by default, Raven.

Later, on the plane, Sebastian turned to Raven. "Your brother really does look out for you. Do all four of you get along as well as you two do?" Try as he might, the questions poured out of him like a kettle's steam. It was impossible to spend time with someone without asking a question or two.

She nodded, looking out the small window. "Pretty much. There's a big difference in age between Wren, the oldest, and Lark, who is still in college, and Robin and me in the middle. But yes, we do. Maybe one day you can meet the other two. Robin and her husband are expecting their first baby in December."

Watching the clouds out the window, he realized he would love to spend the holidays around Raven's family. He liked Wren and wondered if the others were like him. The wistfulness in Raven's tone did not hide the delight when she mentioned her sister was pregnant. She needed to spend more time with her family. And his parents as well, if he had anything to do with it.

He'd have to check and see what his parents planned on doing around the holidays this year. Since he was away so much, sometimes they closed the house and flew to Mexico for some sunshine. At other times, Dad would haul out boxes of lights and decorate the house to look like a gingerbread cottage, and Mom would bake up a small storm. One never knew what they might decide to do.

Back on solid ground, Sebastian pushed the cart loaded with their luggage out to the long-term parking.

They halted beside a rusty, late-model sedan. "This is your car?" she asked, glancing between him and the car.

He paused, wondering how his car appeared to someone else. It had two different colored side-panel fenders, and the two doors were both different colors altogether. He'd forgotten which one was the original one. Rust seemed to be the predominant color left on the original parts.

"Yeah."

"I've never seen so many colors on one vehicle. Looks like a bad patchwork quilt."

He made the attempt to look insulted but failed miserably. "Yep. It spends a lot of time sitting in airport parking lots," he explained, stacking the cases and duffel bags in the trunk. "Rattletraps like this tend to go unnoticed by thieves compared to sleek new beauties."

She giggled. "Unnoticed? I'd think it would frighten a thief. Bet they think if they tried to break in, it would fall apart before they could finish the job."

Grinning, he slammed the trunk. She winced, her expression saying she was waiting for something to fall off.

"You could be right," he acknowledged. "Either way, it's dependable even if it's not pretty to look at. Care to try your luck?"

She gazed innocently around the lot. "Well," she said slowly, "since all I see are sleek new beauties, I guess I have to take my chances with this, um, relic. I assume it's the multitude of bumper stickers that hold it together, right?"

Unable to hide his amusement, despite her deadpan quip, he pulled her door open. "She might take offense at your comments," he whispered loudly. "I call her Betty."

"I do hope you are kidding." She arched an eyebrow.

"I am."

Pulling out of the parking lot, she suddenly punched his arm. "You had me worried for a second there."

"Now, I'd never call a car by the name Betty," he assured, amused at her reaction. "I'd call it Sara Sue." His laughter was rich, full, and felt good to his heart.

After the stress at Gull Island, they both needed something to laugh about. Now, he needed to find something for Raven to find amusement in.

———

As Sebastian drove them through town, heading into the suburban outskirts, Raven watched the houses change from rows of apartments to nice townhouses to cookie-cutter planned developments. They turned into an upscale development with sprawling houses boasting manicured lawns beneath blankets of white and stately ornaments. All that was missing were the black wrought iron fences.

"Tell me about your parents." She fidgeted with her hands, unable to find somewhere to keep them still.

He shrugged. "Mom's mom, she dotes on me much like Wren does with you," he said, cutting her a grin. "Dad is dad. Being an only kid, I pretty much can do no wrong in their eyes, and I've always thought they were pretty neat parents."

"Always?"

He considered that. "Well, there was a time, a few years ago, back when I was a teenager, when I wasn't so impressed with them. But eventually, we worked past our differences." He grinned. "They forgave me for my young and foolish ideas. I forgave them for their strict and domineering ways."

How nice to have grown up with two parents, she thought wistfully. Wren was both brother and parent to her because of their three-year age difference. There were fifteen years between Wren and Lark, so she felt more like a mother to Lark than a sister.

"So why do you still live at home with them?"

He shrugged, turning into the drive of a pale yellow house. "Just easier. I'm not home enough to warrant spending money on an apartment or house, so I pay them to collect my mail and store my stuff. I blow in occasionally, hang out a bit, and blow back out again. Mom likes it because she can cook healthy meals for me, ensure my laundry is done correctly, and at least make sure she has fulfilled her motherly duties until the next trip. Dad and I might take in a game if there's time, have a cookout or something we enjoy." Stopping, he shifted the car into park. "Okay, we're here. Are you ready?"

She blew out an uneven breath, looking at the elegant house. At the front entry with the brass knocker and kick plate on the door, her hands worked the hem of her shirt. "I guess so."

He laughed. "Come on, my brave one. They won't eat you."

CHAPTER
ELEVEN

Sebastian had his mother's green eyes, Raven decided immediately. As beautiful as they were on him, they were more stunning on a woman. No wonder his father had fallen in love with her. The maternal side of the family's beguiling green eyes. What an unfair advantage.

Donna, as his mother immediately insisted on being called, wrapped Raven with a warm embrace.

"Here, let me help you with that," Sebastian's father suggested, taking her coat once introductions were made. Tall, handsome, and graying well, David wore a pleasant smile and offered an infectious laugh.

"Sebastian, you've been hurt," Donna pointed out in dismay, assessing the bandage that showed once he had removed his coat.

"No big deal, Mom. Lost a fight is all."

Raven gasped. "The more accurate truth is he won a fight...while protecting me."

His dad rubbed his chin, much like she had seen Sebastian do a couple of times. "I believe there is a story in there we want to hear. Let's go into the living room to hear this properly. Good to have you home again, son," his dad added, clapping a hand on his shoulder, following them. "How long are you here for?"

Raven could see the desire in both their eyes for their son to stay awhile, and a definite interest in her. Did he often show up back home with an unknown girl in tow?

"Not too long," Sebastian replied, sitting next to Raven, taking her hand, a move both his parents caught. A warmth rushed through her at the comforting touch.

"Raven is visiting from Gull Island, and I have to get her back home before too terribly long." He slid her a smile. "She has a big brother who might not like it if I keep her away past his idea of curfew."

Her cheeks heated at the comment, and she knew they must be pink. David chuckled at Sebastian's joke, as did Donna, heading into the kitchen. His smile widened.

She could tell Wren liked Sebastian enough not to send the cavalry if she were gone for what he considered too long a period.

"I think we are safe from Wren's protective tendencies for now," she replied, wishing she had worn something lighter weight. She was noticing how much warmer Connecticut was than her island home.

His mother returned with tea service and little cakes. Pouring the tea into a bone china teacup, she handed one to Raven and one to her husband. Raven was surprised when she popped a soda can and poured it into another teacup, handing it to Sebastian.

"So, that's the island our son went to for his latest assignment," David said thoughtfully. "We thought it was uninhabited. Just an old light station."

"I live in the house at that light station. I rent it from the Coast Guard."

"Raven's the most current keeper of the Gull Island Lighthouse. And you won't believe our story." Setting his soda aside, he took her hand and launched into their adventure.

Raven listened to Sebastian's recap, interjecting as needed, keenly watching his parents' expressions.

"Well, Raven," his dad finally said, "it seems to me the dog was the best form Sebastian could have shifted into. It suited every need for you and the island."

She sought Donna's eyes, hoping to see her doubts mirrored back to her. She saw compassion instead. Concern but no doubts. How odd, to be sitting here discussing Sebastian's shapeshifting so casually with his parents, as if they were discussing next week's weather forecast.

"Well, Dad, the dog might've been the best form, I just wish I had handled it a little differently," Sebastian admitted, sliding that look to her again. The bewitching green eyes full of concern and unspoken emotions, hot enough to melt her heart, while still apologetic for his crime of deceit.

David scoffed. "It got the job done. You must return to testify in the trial. Make it a priority, Son."

"Such a lovely name, Raven," Donna observed quietly. "So, what do you do out in that cold isolation? I hear it's cool there even in the summer."

"I, ah, paint," she faltered. "I am a self-taught painter. And it does stay cooler in the summer."

"She's brilliant. Her newest works should be on display in a gallery."

"Next to your photographs? I suppose they would make a great exhibit paired together."

A chill slithered up Raven's spine at the innocent suggestion. They would look great side by side. Except neither form needed to be shared with the public.

"Maybe," Sebastian hedged.

"You should show Raven the ones you have in the

nearby museum. I do hope you plan on taking her out while you're here?"

"Of course."

———

Hours later, alone in a strange bed, Raven stared up at the ceiling. Unconsciously, she listened for the reassuring chimes of the Grandfather clock from downstairs, the wind whistling past the tower, or the waves splashing onto the rocky shore. Here, now in the darkness, an unfamiliar silence greeted her.

Giving up any pretense of sleep, she went to the window. With no cushioned window seat inviting her, she stood, using her back to hold the curtain open, with her arms at her side. Wishing to see the pale moonlight spilling through the heavy clouds, instead, she saw only darkness, save the measured artificial lights of the utility poles. Had she been wrong to come? Wrong to leave her island home? Wren and that darn treasure hadn't left her much choice. Why had Madeline even bothered to show it to her and Sebastian, now of all times?

Turning her back to the urban nightscape, she returned to bed. Sebastian's parents were wonderful. Polite, accepting, and quite likeable. When his dad slid that very same look to his mom, it always stilled her heart. She knew she could easily learn to love his family.

But there was another matter, her conscience argued. Alone in the kitchen, washing up the dishes, she had confided in his mother. Now, alone in the dark, she replayed the scene back in her mind.

"Doesn't it bother you, his ability to change?" she had asked.

Donna shook her head. "Not at all. I consider it a

wonderful and thoughtful gift from someone who once saved my son. I think of how much it has enriched his life over the years, giving him unparalleled advantages with his photography, and quite simply adding joy to his life. I can only see it as a wonderful asset."

She mulled that over, the things she had yet to see for herself. "I suppose I've only experienced the shock of it. And worse, the deception that came with it."

Donna chuckled. "Now, to be completely honest, I am rather glad he received this gift later as an adult instead of as a young child." Her eyes sparkled like jade. "Can you imagine the grief he would have caused me while growing up if he could've shifted back then?"

No, not really. She could not imagine living full-time around someone who could morph into any animal at any time, let alone raising a child with the ability.

"He was always so curious as a young boy," Donna went on with a whimsical smile, holding a plate aloft. "Always asking questions and wanting to know everything about everything."

Raven grinned, her own scrubbing having halted as well. Apparently, he hadn't changed that much over the years. They both sat down at the small table, their dish duty temporarily halted. Raven saw this as a good opportunity to dig deeper into his mom's true feelings about his magic skill.

"But what if he deceived someone while shifted? Not telling someone who he really was? What could he really do?"

Donna rested her hands on the table and studied Raven for a moment. Long enough to make her uncomfortable, and she wished she could recall the questions.

"In that case, if that happened, I would have to think he did what he felt was best at the time. I trust Sebastian to be discreet about his shapeshifting and not to misuse his special ability."

Now, in the darkness of her room, the words haunted her. The honesty of his mother's words poked at her.

———

"I was thinking we could head to the museum downtown," Sebastian casually mentioned over breakfast. "We could see some sights and maybe catch a show while we are at it?"

"Sounds fine," she agreed.

He beamed with a huge smile. "Great. We can consider it a date of sorts."

Later, Sebastian parked his pitiful jalopy in the parking garage downtown. They strolled along the sidewalk with their arms linked.

"You've really made an impression on my folks."

"Really?" That was nice to know.

"Yes, Dad was telling me that it was about time I spent quality time around a woman like you. And Mom pointed out you have rare qualities that deserve my attention."

She stopped, gazing up at him. "They both said all that?"

"They did. And like an obedient child, I plan to do just that."

She giggled, stepping forward once more. As Raven entered the museum, she could tell he was very familiar with the place. Patrons and employees alike warmly greeted him, some patting his arm affectionately and commenting on his works or recent awards. A few sent her ill-disguised, curious glances. He made quick and vague introductions, as if respecting her desire to remain in the background. This was his world, his life, and his people. She was just a visitor.

"I should warn you about Abby," he said, as they rode

the elevator to the second floor. "She's the author who writes those inspirational little things that accompany many of the photos. You might have noticed them in the *Winters* book?"

"I did see a few."

"Good. You'll notice a few more here. Not all the photographs have them, but the ones that needed a voice, Abby was able to put a voice to them."

The elevator doors opened, and they stepped into a huge room with a vaulted ceiling. Natural lighting streamed in from all directions. Rows upon rows of photographs, paintings, and drawings lined the walls.

"Here, mine are set up over this way." Taking her elbow, he escorted her slowly along the displays until they reached a banner heralding his name. He stayed slightly behind her, waiting patiently and quietly as she slowly studied each picture. Finally, he stopped, leaning against a wall with his arms folded, as she circled the exhibit. She could've chuckled at his anxious facial expression as he waited for her feedback.

They were, in a word, perfect. Unlike the winter-themed pictures in his 'Winters' book, these seemed to follow no set theme. They were shot all over the world, at all times of the year. Some were as simple as a dragonfly on a flower, drenched in color. Others were as complex as cascading waterfalls in a lush green jungle with brightly colored parrots and brown monkeys overhead. Her breath left in a startled gasp as she came to a halt. This one was the best. The simplest.

He photographed a natural spring in a field. That was all. A few old trees stood sentry in the background. Gazing into the picture, Raven could almost feel the wind caressing her cheeks, smell the scent of wildflowers on that warm breeze, and hear the gurgling of the bubbling water. So simple. She could just about walk into the picture and touch the cool water with her fingertips, grab a leaf from the trees, or feel the tall field grass bending beneath her feet. The natural water would taste sweet on her tongue. Wet and refreshing. Unbidden, she leaned closer, only then noticing a plaque.

> *From deep within ourselves,*
> *hope springs eternally.*
> *~Abigail Turner~*

"How beautiful," she said, thinking the picture and the words were a perfect match. The water bubbling up from deep within the ground, a perfect image for the hope that lives in one's heart. The hope that Sebastian has tapped into and caused to flow once more.

His arms curled around her waist. "Do you like it?" His breath heated her neck.

She nodded, amazed at how her body responded, yielding and folding into his. Heat spiraled through her, not unlike the water bubbling in the photo. "I love it. Where was it taken?"

"Iowa. Last fall."

Turning to him, she thought of all the places he had seen. So many testified in this room. Her thoughts of his wandering warred for space of his touch. Heat turned to need, startling her. Then he kissed her.

She stiffened, emitting a startled breath. Heat sliced through her, pouring steadily down to her toes. Her hands reached up, encircling his neck as she relaxed against him. He tasted good, so good. Sweet. Fresh like the bubbling spring. She closed her eyes, feeling herself slipping away. Her fingers laced into his hair. She held on as he carried her on a delicious journey.

Sebastian cupped her chin with his fingertips, tilting her face. Dipping down, he pressed his lips over hers, plunging forward, risking any thorns.

He swallowed back a happy groan as she surrendered without a fight, yielding to him, welcoming him. Her hands in his hair excited him, further arousing him as she slipped her fingers beneath his shirt, spreading them over his ribs. He drew her close, tasting the fire on her tongue. Her heat covered him. He sensed her need. Eyes closed, he knew he could die a satisfied man.

Finally, regretfully, he pulled away, breath coming in pants. Oh, yeah, she was something. Intoxicating. She tasted like wild honey. Licking his lips, he was already hungry for another taste. Her eyes were hooded, and her lips were swollen and wet. Taking another breath, he plunged, hungry for that honey-sweet taste.

"Sebastian, hey man."

Whirling, he spotted his friend Greg, standing nearby and wearing an amused grin. Burning hot, he placed some open air between himself and Raven, retaining a grip on her waist. Later, he promised himself he'd return to that wild and exotic sweetness of her lips.

"Greg, what's up?" he asked, trying for casual, knowing he was failing miserably. Oh well. Like Greg had never kissed a girl.

"I didn't know you were back in town. I just happened to stop in, and here you are." His lips twitched as he barely controlled his amusement, eyes flickering to Raven.

"Raven, meet my friend Greg. Greg, this is Raven. She's visiting for a few days."

Greg extended his hand. "Nice to meet you," he said, before turning to Sebastian.

"Seb, you know that benefit concert tomorrow night for the McGuire family? Well, Tom called out sick. He has a big, bad bug and is really out of it. So we need another sax player."

"Sax player?" Raven asked with a perky voice.

Before Sebastian could explain, Greg jumped in. "Yes, Seb here is part of our jazz and blues band. He's our main songwriter and one of our sax and guitar players. I play bass," he said, jabbing a finger at himself. "We had set up this benefit concert for a local family in need for tomorrow." He shifted his gaze to Sebastian.

"We're starting and ending the playlist with your two newest songs," he added, hopeful.

"Why hadn't you planned to be part of it originally?" she asked him.

"I hadn't planned on being here right now. I'm still supposed to be on the island."

With a bright smile at the men, she stated, "How lucky we ended up coming back here instead. Isn't that great? Now you can play after all. It sounds like a very worthy event."

Relief and puzzlement swept over him equally. He noticed she wasn't surprised about his being in a band or a songwriter. "Are you planning on coming too?" He tilted his head at her.

"I love a good jazz concert. What an unexpected treat."

———

Leaving the museum, Raven linked her arm through his. They dodged some rush-hour pedestrians crowding the sidewalks, pouring in and out of buildings. Raven had forgotten how congested the streets and walkways could get at certain times of day.

"I like Greg. Are all your friends like him?"

"Pretty much. We're just a bunch of guys who enjoy getting together and playing music. They're nice enough to allow me to write most their songs and even play a little music with them."

His humble explanation touched her. She'd bet he was a bigger, more important part of the band than he let on. Heat glowed inside her, like a fireplace, as she thought of that night in the gazebo and his work in progress inside that little black notebook. If only he knew she knew about both of them. Dare she mention she heard him play that night? "So what's the name of your band?"

"The Night Thieves."

"I like that."

"Wasn't my idea. Our trumpet and trombone players came up with the name. I wanted to go with—"

"Oh, my word," a woman's excited voice rang out, startling them. "Excuse me, but you're Raven Pembrooke, aren't you?"

Raven turned, horror uncurling in her chest. A woman of about her age stood before her, face alight with joy. Waving her finger in Raven's face, she continued loudly, "I can't believe it. Raven Pembrooke, right here in our town. Where have you been all this time? Are you returning to work?"

Raven ducked her head, covering her face, as the instant dread swept over her. "You're mistaken," she muttered, trying to dodge the woman. "I'm not who you think I am."

Sebastian tried his best to guide her along the sidewalk, but the crowd was thick, and the woman persisted. Her loud voice ringing and gathering the glances of others. People stopped to stare. Raven darted him a glance and read the obvious puzzlement on his face. She broke into a cold sweat. The sweat dripped along her spine and between her breasts. Her heart was pounding loudly enough for all to hear.

She nervously scanned for somewhere to escape, but there were too many people. The doors to the shops were clogged with displays and people. Taking another few steps, she noticed the woman pressed closer. Her head was light with dizziness from the sheer force of the woman.

"Are you here to start shooting again, Raven? What happened with you and—"

"I am not who you think I am," she insisted, coming to a halt. "Please stop."

Undeterred, the woman waved her finger in Raven's face again. "Oh *yes,* you are. I know that face. What's it been? Five years since—"

"Lady," he addressed her coolly while pushing Raven behind him for protection. "She said she isn't who you think she is. Go on now." He pointed one finger away from them.

Reluctantly, she walked away, carrying on about Raven Pembrooke being in town. Breathing a sigh of relief, Raven leaned into his supporting embrace.

"Wow, thanks for that. Let's get out of here, please," she said, heart throbbing as she watched the woman retreat.

Taking her hand, Sebastian nodded and guided her as they walked through the throngs of pedestrians. "What was that all about?"

"Nothing. I don't know. Some crazy woman on the loose."

CHAPTER
TWELVE

Donna Knight loved to shop. Taking her around town, they hit every retail store within a twenty-mile radius. Maybe more. But it was fun. Donna possessed a fine sense of humor, which she had seen glimpsed in her son.

"Well, what do you think so far?" Donna asked, guiding them into a small café.

Raven dropped her packages and then herself onto a comfortable chair, almost breathless with the pace. "It's been wonderfully crazy," she replied, smiling.

"I love honesty," Donna stated, returning the cordial smile, and plucked a menu. "Fortunately for us, Sebastian has to practice for tomorrow, leaving us some time to get you something nice to wear."

She not only had a nice dress and shoes for the concert tomorrow night, but she also had lightweight shirts to wear during her stay, rather than bulky sweaters and thermals. At first, she was sorry to have mentioned that all she had packed was cold-weather gear. She was glad for the time spent shopping. Overwhelmed at first, swept away by the action, she soon caught herself enjoying the expert way

Donna charged into the stores, like she was charging into battle. She conquered and took only the goods she wanted. It was as if she were a conquering Viking. She had never shopped like that before.

"My husband says I was born to shop," Donna said with eyes sparkling in amusement. "He says he cringes every time I say I feel a retail fever coming on."

Raven laughed as the waitress came and took their orders for tea and sandwiches. "My treat, Raven," Donna assured her. "This has been a great chance for us to get to know one another. You and Sebastian seem like a good match," she declared. "But his ability bothers you."

Raven squirmed. "A little. I think it's more about how he deceived me. No matter how I feel about him, I still feel I can't fully trust him." The words tumbled out, and she held her breath. Should she have been so blatantly honest with his mother?

Donna nodded. She cast her look briefly around the room before coming back to rest on Raven. "I can see where you could feel that way. Perhaps he could have handled the situation better. I don't know. I wasn't there and you were. But I do know two things for sure. You two clearly have feelings for each other. Anyone can see that. And despite anything else, you can fully trust him."

Those words, spoken so honestly, knocked the air from her lungs. Not knowing what else to say, she nodded.

"Now, tell me about this lighthouse you stay at," Donna requested.

"There isn't anything there except the light station built back in the 1800s. There's my house, which is a big Victorian, and the outbuildings and the light tower. The rest of the island is woods, rocks, and the wildlife that lives there. Deer, bear, wolves, raccoon, oh, and a ghost named Madeline."

Donna paused, sandwich midair, her fascinated smile fading. "You have a ghost for company?"

Raven shrugged. "Not so much for company. She just hangs around sometimes. She never talks and is harmless."

Donna's look bordered on incredulous, so Raven continued. "I came across Madeline's journal, written before she died, and her mother's journal, which continued for several more years. Madeline was a teenager, and her death was quite accidental. Her mother was distraught and only wanted to leave the island after her daughter's death. It was a hard life back then."

Donna grinned, thinking it over. "Seriously, it doesn't sound a whole lot easier now. You are quite brave. All alone, with just the wild animals and a harmless ghost. I could never do that. Honestly, where are the retail stores?"

They both broke into peals of laughter.

Sebastian unhooked his sax, dismantled and carefully packed it away. He was ready for the concert. One drawback to being away so much was all the practice he missed with the band. While he played when out on assignments as often as he could, he tended to do more writing while on the road instead, leaving the real playing for those few and far between visits home.

Hopefully, his mom wasn't wearing Raven out. Once home, he made himself a sandwich, thinking back on Raven's startled expression when his mom suggested a little shopping while he practiced. Yeah, he knew his mom's idea of a little shopping. It had been what...almost three hours already. He hoped she liked to shop.

Which led him to a new thought. What did he really know about her? A lot, but not her past. Even her confessions when he was Salzburg did not shed much light on her past life before Gull Island. The woman on the street earlier was certain she knew Raven. And about her past. What did she ask? Was Raven here to start shooting again? Shooting what? She had expressed no interest in his camera equipment.

Finished eating his sandwich, he checked the time. He could hop onto the computer and do some basic research. If she were recognizable enough for someone to spot her on the street, she should be listed somewhere on the internet.

Feeling a tiny bit dirty, he fired up the computer and logged in. Breath catching, he typed her name into the search bar. *Raven Pembrooke.*

Several results popped up. Scanning them, he clicked the most recent, dated five years ago.

Startled by what he read, he eagerly clicked two more result links. The accompanying pictures in the articles were stunning. He would never have guessed this outcome. Adrenaline coursing through him, he read the remaining result links, drinking in the words and images.

Thankful to be sitting, because there was some uncertainty he couldn't stand. He logged off the computer. Glaring at the blank screen, he worked his mind around the articles, documents, and photos. *Um, wow.*

He continued to slowly mull over the information. He could not turn back the hands of time for Raven. He had no way to replace what was now gone. But he could...gently fingering his bracelet, he touched the familiar leather, turned it, and wondered. *Can I?*

———

Raven felt like a princess. The taffeta dress, in multiple shades of blue, featured ruffles that flowed to the floor, fitting her perfectly. Donna had chosen well. She loved the silky feel of the fabric as it rustled against her skin. She hadn't missed the surprised light dancing in Sebastian's eyes as she descended the staircase, as they prepared to leave for the concert.

"Raven," he drawled slowly, "you look lovely. That dress becomes you."

Nodding her head, unable to hide her smile of pleasure, she murmured a polite thank you.

Arriving at the hall where the concert was booked, he handed her over to his dad, giving Raven a wink.

"Watch her, Dad. I'd hate to have to fight some boys off when we're done tonight."

"Fighting some boys off might be good for him," he replied as Sebastian strolled away. He smiled and winked at Raven.

Blushing, she settled in with his parents in the second row back from the front, hands drumming her knees as they waited. She couldn't really believe she was here, with Sebastian's parents and listening to a jazz concert he was playing in. Excitement coursed through her as she waited.

Soon her toes tapped the floor impatiently.

The buzz from others seated around them stirred her, reminding her of other times she attended concerts, plays, fashion shows, and art exhibitions.

It struck her what she'd missed from five years of self-created isolation. Public events used to mean so much to her social well-being.

"Are you all right, honey?" Donna asked, leaning over.

"Hmmm? Yes, I'm fine. Just lost in thoughts, I guess. This is unbelievable to be here and soon to hear Sebastian and his band."

Donna patted her knee, smiling.

Occasionally, random strands of music drifted up from

behind the heavy curtain as the musicians tuned their instruments and did a sound check. The seats filled as people arrived, conversing quietly among themselves or with friends who joined them, raising the gentle buzz to a steady drone of laughter and whispers.

The emcee strolled onto the stage, thanking the visitors for their time and generous spirits, recapping the nature of the benefit. He introduced the band that organized the concert and donated their time and talents for the family. "The Night Thieves," he concluded amid thunderous applause.

The curtain fell away, showing eight men gathered on the stage. Heart beating rapidly, Raven searched for Sebastian. She spotted Greg standing with his bass, while other members sat at the drums, the piano, a trumpet, a trombone, and then there was Sebastian with his shiny saxophone. One more member stood alone at a microphone holding a clarinet. The music began. Raven was drawn into the song.

Rich, deep tones filled the room as they played a slow song. The lead singer belted out a tune about love on the rocks. Realizing this was one Sebastian had written, she noticed how similar the song was to the ones she had read in his notebook. An eager chill coursed over her body. The song was beautiful and haunting. Watching him, how his fingers stroked the keys, his eyelids lowered in concentration, a warmth filled her. A yearning. His foot tapped in rhythm along with the others, his expression full of pleasure and pride. He appeared to be lost in the music and the moment.

The song ended, and they moved to a jazzier, upbeat number. Stage lights sparkled off the instruments as they swayed, rocked, and tapped to the beat. The singer belted out a happy song, with the bass, drums, and piano players providing harmony.

This evening's performance and company were absolutely perfect. The whole package of being out with his parents and watching Sebastian perform. His music was beyond words. Everything was undeniably picture-perfect.

———

After the third song, Sebastian risked a glance at Raven. Would she be enjoying the music? Would he be able to return his attention to playing after taking the risky glance? Heart throbbing, he sought her out within the crowd. She sat with his parents and belonged with them. She was comfortable with his parents and fit in well, as if she were a member of the family. Her excited smile told him she enjoyed the performance. The smoky blue dress was a fantastic color on her. The fabric was as silky smooth as her skin under his fingertips. She was stunning. He was struggling to keep his eyes and mind on the task at hand.

Stroking the sax keys, as they started another song, he wished he were stroking her shoulders while tipping her head to bring their lips together. Heaven help him, but he was going to have to kiss her very soon. Drawing his attention to the sheet music before him, he struggled to find his place.

He shouldn't have risked looking at her, but the view was worth falling behind the band. He might get ribbed about it later from the guys, but he didn't care. Those few moments of seeing her pleasure were more than worth it.

———

By the sixth song, Raven determined Sebastian had a poet's soul and a musician's skill. He could have easily pursued a career in music as he had in photography. The band worked well together, shifting from soulful, teary ballads to up-tempo, jazzy struts and incorporating a bluesy number as well. Clearly, they were not only good friends but also band members. She wondered about their history. Did any of them know about Sebastian's shifting skill? She hated that such a preoccupation had to pepper her thoughts, but the niggling thought crept in despite her best efforts not to dwell on the matter.

The band stopped for a break, and the emcee came back on stage, asking for a round of applause while the curtain drifted shut. In the crowd, people resumed chatting, exchanging opinions about the music and other topics.

Suddenly, Raven spotted Sebastian and two other band members coming onto the floor, weaving their way through the rows of chairs. Heart drumming, she waited for his approach, eager to tell him how much she enjoyed the music.

A willowy redhead seemingly materialized out of nowhere, like a specter, stepping into his arms. She delivered a peck on the cheek, laughing as he whispered something in her ear. Seeing him take her hands into his, sparks knifed through Raven. Her jaw dropped and her eyes widened as her cheeks heated.

Who was the woman? Old girlfriend? Current girl-friend? Dare she mention it to his parents? Surely, they recognized her.

Casting a lowered glance at Donna, the older woman had also noticed the redhead's hold on Sebastian. From her tight-lipped expression, Raven would have to guess she did not care for either the display or the woman. Interest battled with embarrassment as she forced herself to look away.

Forget about him fighting the boys away. She had no intention of fighting the women.

Greg grabbed his arm, peeling the woman's manacles off his arm, and pulled him toward the stage, where the two disappeared behind the curtain. It seemed the time allotted for their break was finished.

Raven watched as the woman returned to a chair, a satisfied smile on her face, whispering to the woman seated beside her. Tasting a sourness in her mouth, she fidgeted during the second half of the concert. Barely able to watch Sebastian, she kept her eyes on the other members instead. She could not wait for the event to end.

"Raven, is everything okay?" David whispered.

Now even more embarrassed, to add to her anger, Raven forced her jaw to relax. "Yes, I'm fine." She rolled her shoulders, working the tension out. She unclenched her fists, wondering at what point she'd gripped them.

"Fine." She repeated, forcing a smile, as if to say "see". She probably looked like she was grimacing in distress.

David shook his head, and she knew he wasn't convinced but chose to let the conversation go.

Raven was grateful when the Night Thieves finished their set. She looked around for the red-haired woman, but she seemed to have gone away. Good riddance.

"We can wait out in the foyer." David gently took her elbow and Donna's and steered them toward the entryway. Raven happily breathed in cool drafts of fresh air each time someone left, and air entered the building. She considered asking how much longer but felt that would be rude and childish.

Finally, Sebastian made his way through the crowd. He

moved up next to Raven, and she sidled closer to the door. Still no sign of the red-haired woman. Good.

"So how did everyone enjoy the concert?" he asked, taking another step toward her.

She eagerly followed his dad out to the car, where she could pretend to be interested in anything other than Sebastian and see the red-haired woman kissing him.

"Great, of course," Donna said.

"A packed house, which should really help the McGuire family," his dad pointed out.

"Raven? Did you enjoy it?"

"It was fine," she replied coolly, adjusting her sweater over her shoulders as she climbed into the car.

He stowed the sax case and settled next to her. She was probably overreacting, but why bother inviting her to come home with him, meet his family and friends, ask her to come to the concert, and then kiss the red-headed woman? If they were a thing, she wished he'd just tell her.

But then again, Sebastian Knight had been known for not being forthcoming with important information.

———

Raven thanked her hosts and pleaded for an early night upon their return home. She stood at the bedroom window watching the city lights come on as darkness slowly fell.

She had no right to be jealous, but she was. Wishing Madeline were there, she ached for someone to talk to about her feelings. Considering going to Donna, she decided against it. They had laid the groundwork for friendship, but she did not think it was sturdy enough for this sort of discussion about her son.

Watching the redhead ooze into Sebastian's arms like an octopus attaching its tentacles had unleashed a sense of hostility she'd never felt. Unlike simple anger, it bordered on something she couldn't name. And to make it worse, he had made no effort to remove her from himself until his friend pulled him away. He even whispered in her ear. Something good enough to make her laugh.

How dare he!

She slapped the curtain closed and paced the room. Perhaps it was time for her to return home to Gull Island. Alone. Return to her former life before everyone had invaded her and the island.

Yes. True, she'd enjoyed some community events, and it rekindled when she had a full social calendar. But that was before. And this is now. She needed to return. Tomorrow, she would speak to Sebastian.

———

After breakfast, Raven announced, "I want to return home."

Sebastian almost dropped his coffee cup. He'd been wrapped up trying to figure out what happened with Raven last night. The visit home had been going great. Initially, she seemed to enjoy the concert, but once it ended, she withdrew into herself with the prickly thorns out again. And now, she was breaking her silence with another heart-stopping bombshell declaration.

"Why now? Aren't you having a good time here?" *What did I miss? Or misread so badly?*

"I was. Now I would prefer to go home."

He hesitated, taking in her tight-lipped expression, the storm clouds in her eyes, and the color in her cheeks.

"You needn't trouble yourself. I can make it there myself. If you can simply take me to the airport, I'll be fine."

"Raven," he said, holding in a sigh at her cool, detached

tone. At her avoidance. She was determined not to look at him for more than a few minimal seconds. Yes, he had complete confidence she would be 'fine'. "Don't be silly. I will be more than happy to go back with you. I just hadn't thought it would be so soon. What with the cargo deal and all." He hesitated again. "I had thought you were enjoying yourself."

"I was." Defiance crept into her voice. "Now I—"

"Okay, I get it. Can you tell me what brought this on?"

She silently regarded him with her arms folded across her chest. What was the point?

"Okay, fine. Can you at least tell me if you enjoyed yourself last night? At the concert?"

The storm clouds darkened. Sebastian could swear he almost saw smoke swirling around her head. Ah, he deduced, now there was the problem. How should he go about fixing it? He almost shrugged his shoulders, not sure which way to handle this.

"Let's take a walk," he quietly suggested, daring to reach and touch her folded arms. She stiffened.

"Why?" she pulled away.

"Because I asked you to."

Patience, Knight. She's as fragile as she's tough.

In silent acquiescence, she reached for her jacket at the doorway, making sure he knew she was capable of handling everything.

He yielded to her, nodded his head out to the driveway, and fell into step beside her, his hands curled into his pockets.

There was a small park for the subdivision residents that he headed toward. A small plot of grassy land, with a set of swings, a tennis court, a few benches, and a child-sized merry-go-round. Once they passed through the wrought-iron gate, he headed for a bench, glad to spot no one else around. A few small birds twittered about the tree branches. Raven headed for the swings, settling on a seat and kicking off with a foot.

"Do you like swings?" He watched her for a moment. "Or is it just a convenient way to avoid sitting next to me?"

Startled at his directness, she regarded him, kicking harder to gain height. "Both."

He crossed his arms as he leaned against the pole to watch her swing. She did have a youthful delight in the swinging motion, except she was too upset to completely enjoy it. Filing the note aside in his mind, he moved on to the bigger problem. It was something about the show.

"So, what did you think about the concert?"

Her head snapped up. Her eyes remained stormy. "The music was fine. You all played well. How long have you been a band?"

His heart swelled at her sincere praise. "About ten years. We started as a garage band at the drummer's house."

She hesitated. "Do they know about you? Your..."

He bit his inside cheek to keep from smiling as she stumbled over his shapeshifting ability.

"My shifting? No, they don't. Ironically, I had to shift once, and they never figured it was me."

"Don't you feel bad for deceiving them?"

Oh, but when she struck with those thorns, she could jab them hard. No wonder Wren just backed off now.

"What do you want me to say? Yes, I'm a jerk and a heel for not sharing that with them. But would it be something they would believe or understand? If the time ever came that they needed to know, I'd share it. Right now, it's best if I don't tell them." He paused, taking a breath. "That is the way I have decided to live with my ability. Now, the question is, can you accept me this way?"

"Why should I have to accept you or not accept you? Why does it matter either way?"

"Because I—" Catching himself, he paused. Wishing she would stop swinging. Wishing he could pull her into his arms. He accepted that neither was going to happen right away.

"Raven, look, I'm crazy about you. I care about you a lot. I don't know what upset you last night, but I wish you would talk to me about your discomfort."

He watched her frown, listened to her deep, huffy breath, and drag her feet to a stop. He glanced at her hands as they tightened an already firm grip around the swing's plastic-coated chains. He wanted to pull her into his arms and kiss her troubled, irritated look away.

"Who was that red-haired woman?"

He could not imagine or brace himself for this unexpected question.

CHAPTER
THIRTEEN

Sebastian couldn't have imagined or braced himself for this unexpected question. *This* is what had Raven so prickly all of a sudden?

Darn his bad luck. Sebastian swallowed back an oath. How had he missed the signs? Why hadn't he considered the source of her quick change of behavior? Her sudden cool indifference. She was jealous of Diana.

He replayed last night in his mind, running the hours by in a fast reel. Beside him, Raven waited, brow puckered and toes tapping the ground. Yep, jealous.

His intention last night had been to see Raven and his parents during the band's break. He even planned on planting a quick kiss on Raven's cheek. Instead, he was intercepted by Diana and couldn't get away. To keep her hands off of him, he'd held them in his own, looking for an escape. She wasn't one for taking hints, subtle or otherwise. He had hoped his reminder growl would cool her down, but instead, it seemed to have the opposite effect. Her girlish little laughter grated his nerves like nails on a chalkboard.

He had felt ready to snap when Greg tugged him back-stage before he could get to Raven. Now, he could only imagine what it looked like from her chair. He reached to rake through his hair but caught himself. Stuffing his hands back in his pockets, he faced her where she waited on the stopped swing.

"Her name is Diana DeLong."

"That figures. She looked how a Diana DeLong would look."

He found no amusement in her snide comment. Genuinely curious, he asked, "How would a Diana DeLong look?"

She shot him a withering glance before huffing. "All willowy grace and confidence, crowned with that fiery red hair. She doubtlessly has full red lips, gorgeous big eyes, and perfect ivory skin. She probably has a lusty voice and a silken laugh as well. And she would always be perfectly dressed and smell wonderful." She jutted her chin out and gave a flick of her hair over her shoulder.

"She would naturally always say the right thing and never stutter." She paused, eyes narrowing. "The kind of woman all normal women like me dread."

Okay, that was kind of amusing. She was almost describing herself, and he surely never noticed that stuff about Diana. He eyed her white-knuckled grip on the swing cable. Was it possible that prickly Miss Raven Koynes was more than a tiny bit jealous? This enticed him.

"Was or is she your girlfriend?"

Sebastian barely held back a laugh. Girlfriend? Not in a hundred years. "Absolutely not," he declared. "Not in the past, certainly not now, and *definitely* not in the future. Despite what Diana may wish or think."

Raven frowned. "She sure acted like you two were hot last night."

Only one thing had him hot last night, and he was staring at her. "Diana likes to make that look true to others.

Maybe it feeds her fantasy. I don't know." He shrugged. He had no interest in Diana's fantasies. "I cringe every time I run into her, and it's all I can do to keep her off me. I didn't know she was going to be there last night, but I'm not surprised. She follows The Night Thieves around, hoping I'll be playing. Greg came to my rescue to get her away from me. They all do that for me."

"You make her sound almost like a stalker."

He tilted his head to one side. "Yeah, I guess in one sense, she almost is one."

"Maybe you should get a restraining order," she suggested, her tone dry.

"Actually, I have considered that. If I were around more often, I probably would."

"So what brought this...infatuation on?"

"I think it's more like an obsession. About four years ago. She was part of a gallery show in which I received an award. She was the one who presented the plaque. Innocently, I gave her a quick hug and kiss on the cheek. Thrill of the moment kind of thing. Ever since, she's been crazy." So many times since then, he wished he could take that one hug and kiss back.

She swept the park with her gaze, nibbling her bottom lip. Turning back, she asked, "So you're not interested in her?"

This time, he could not hold back the laugh. "No way. I'm not interested in her any more than I was interested in Helen on your island." Why did it seem he attracted the crazy females? Risking more jabs, he approached and removed her hands from the swing and pulled her into his arms. "The only person I am interested in is you, Raven Koynes. No one else. Believe me on that. No. One. Else. But. You."

Hadn't his mother said she could trust him? Looking into his eyes, Raven wanted to believe him. She wanted to wipe away her jealousy and distrust and regain confidence in Sebastian.

He held her gently in his arms. It felt so good, she could have wept with joy. Closing her eyes, she leaned into his shoulder, their hearts beating in rhythm. As he cupped her chin and lifted her face to his, she drank in the emotions in his eyes. Tenderness. Passion. Fire. Her heart hammered faster. He would be true and protect her. She wanted his kiss.

She tilted her head higher in anticipation of the kiss she hungered for. She parted her lips and pressed close.

Sparks ignited within her at their connection. Jolted, she slid her hands to his neck, pressing him closer, and she weaved her fingers into his hair. Melting against his long frame, she eased a happy sigh. His hands tangled in her hair, and she pushed her tongue past his lips, eagerly exploring.

Her hands dipped to his shirt, reaching beneath to skim over his shoulders. His fingers threaded her hair and clasped the back of her neck.

Separating, they stared at each other, panting breathlessly. Warmth coursed through her. "You're right," she said. "Worth the wait."

Chuckling, he took her hand. "Raven, no matter what, you are always worth any wait."

Hand in hand, they headed back to the house. "Do you still want to leave now, or can we stick around a few days? I think my folks like having you around."

"I like them. I guess a few more days won't matter."

She paused, looking around. "Wait, what's that?" She stepped to the side of the road. Listening to a soft cry, head tilted, she spotted something and knelt. "Look. Oh, poor thing."

Scooping a tiny gray bundle of fluff, she cradled it to her chest. "Where do you suppose this baby came from?"

Looking from the little kitten and sweeping the corner where they stood, it was doubtful that the itty-bitty ball of fluff came from either house set back from the street corner.

"Who knows? Someone might've left it here. Harsh, but it happens. People here usually keep their pets inside. I've never seen cats running around loose."

"Oh, you're so tiny. And cold." She turned back to Sebastian. "We must get it warm. Would your parents mind?"

"Here, let me." Taking the cold waif from her grasp, he gently placed it inside his jacket, next to his chest. "I think they'll be okay with this. I also suspect you just adopted a pet."

————

"Well, I guess we have to stay a few more days," Raven stated, disconnecting the call, and handed back the phone Sebastian had loaned her. "We can't get the kitten into the vet until the day after tomorrow, and the airline won't allow it on board without papers from the vet showing the kitten has been vaccinated."

Sebastian wasn't complaining about the new arrangement. "You are going to need a carrier and the supplies for kitty." Now that the little imp was warm, he released it from his shirt. The ball of fluff skittered across the floor, chasing an imaginary toy. Raven giggled at the antic, her laugh sounding musical to him. "And I guess it will need a name as well," he added. Maybe this kitten would be a suitable replacement for the void left by Salzburg.

The kitten climbed onto the sofa, batted at Raven's fingers, arched its back, and raced away, tail lashing as it stopped to tackle Sebastian's toe. Racing away again, it zipped through the legs of the coffee table, pouncing on invisible enemies.

"What a crazy critter," Sebastian commented, amused. Cats were pretty cool, he knew, having experienced their extreme senses and incredible lithe movements. He'd been a cat a few times to gain altitude or proximity for great shots. For such small bundles, they could pack a lot into those furry pounds.

"Kizzy," Raven declared, chasing a few steps to gather the baby to her chest. "That's her name. Crazy kitty. Kizzy."

"Um, I see. Clever. Okay, Kizzy it is."

Sebastian scooped the furry beast from her arms and grinned as it immediately turned on its purr motor. He slashed an eyebrow at Raven. "I think she likes me."

"Good. Your mom and I are going shopping for her necessities. And you can babysit Kizzy."

The kitten nuzzled his hand. "My mom likes you too," Sebastian said, taking a step closer to Raven. "My dad likes you. And I like you."

She swallowed. "You just like me?" Her voice broke as she boldly met his gaze.

He watched as she licked her lips. He bit back a groan. Mercy, but she could tempt him. She wanted a kiss.

He set the kitten down and wrapped his arm around her waist. "Raven, believe it or not, but everyone here is crazy about you. Me most of all."

He claimed her lips in a hot demand. He took possession of her mouth, massaging her tongue. She relaxed in his hold and pressed against his chest. He took that as a green light and buried his fingers in her hair. She arched her back, and a small moan escaped her lips.

She smelled fresh, with a hint of spice, cinnamon, berries, and a hint of jasmine. She smelled of water and wildness. He loved it. She'd not worn it on the island. Had she brought it back to the mainland for this trip?

Regretfully, he pulled back, wetting his own lips, startled to see they were both out of breath. Umm.

"I like the perfume. New?"

"Old." She corrected. "Unearthed it just to come with you."

He ran his tongue over his teeth. "You make me wonder what else you might have unearthed just for this trip."

Raven smiled, big and flirty. "You'll have to wait and find out. Maybe. I have to go find your mom so we can go shopping."

She slowly pulled out of his grasp, their linked fingers the last physical connection. She rubbed her fingertips over his palm as that connection ended. He could honestly say he felt colder without her touch. Until she gave him another flirty wink and grin. His imagination kicked into overdrive, sending warmth spiraling through him.

"Go, Raven, before it's too late and you won't be able to go."

"Take care of my Kizzy," she advised, then her haughty laugh trailed her out of the room.

Sebastian picked up the kitten once more and rubbed his forehead against hers. "Your new mother is something else, kitten."

Left alone with the rambunctious feline, Sebastian twirled a piece of string and tossed a wadded-up scrap of aluminum foil.

"Okay, Kiz, get ready for some real fun. Just to say we did this one time." He felt his bracelet sizzling and the fur growing through his skin. Soon, he was an orange tabby kitten.

On equal terms, they chased each other through the room with lightning speed, rolling, biting, and kicking across the floor, blurry streaks of gray and orange. Feeling the energy and grace only a young cat can possess, Sebastian pounced playfully on the kitten, giving as good as he got from the ball of fluff. Tails puffed, they hissed and spat with wild youthful abandon, clawing one another harmlessly.

Fortunately, he could hold his own with three working legs and held his injured front leg out of the way. He avoided leaping from heights. It worked out that Kizzy could, and they made it work.

Finally, having had enough, his front leg aching and sensing his pal was growing tired, he shifted back to himself.

"Well, Kizzy, that was fun, but don't be expecting it all the time. And don't be telling Raven we did that," he said, donning his clothes again and adjusting the bandage on his arm. Playtime done, he carried the kitten to his room, which doubled as a developing room for his photos. Kizzy jumped onto the bed, circled once, and was immediately asleep.

Since he used an assortment of cameras, he would download the photos from all of them into one file on his computer, where he could look through them in one big order. From there, he could select any or all to print out as preliminary photos for comparison to find the best ones for the assignment.

Sometimes, three slides of the same image could appear nearly identical at first, until printed out, and new details emerge. It was all a process of selecting the best.

Seated at the desk, he dropped the disc of film from all the shots he took at Gull Island onto his computer and opened up the files and studied them with a critical eye.

The very first shots he took while still in the boat were stupendous. The light tower's beacon slicing through the dark clouds, the lightning racing across the sky. He loved them. They truly captured the wild, intense spirit of the moment, reminding him of his aching shoulders, fatigued arms, and the fear of capsizing. Reminding him of the cold wind, the insanely high waves sloshing over the boat, and the bitter cold nipping his neck. They were perfect.

The views of the swelling lake that he took from a beaver's point of view by lying on the ground, before he shifted into the beaver and swam out to the shipwreck, gave another dimensional view of the massive lake. Looking down, looking across, and looking up.

Also, just as lovely were the shots he snapped when Raven showed him around her favorite places. The wildflowers, fall trees, and view from the high meadow. All beautiful and capturing what he had wanted. Well, sort of. Mostly.

Shifting through the sequence of images, his smile faded as he reached the ones of Raven. Standing alone by the old tree on that little spit of rocky ground, wrapped in cold and fog, hair blowing, and angry with him. Sitting on a rock in the meadow, with her head bowed in quiet thought. Walking along the rocky shoreline, the wind tossed her hair like a wild mare's mane. Standing on the widow's walk, staring across the lake's blue-green surface, fingers curled around the railing, her expression dreamy as she silently looked for answers.

His fingers shook as he selected some and hit print.

Heart skipping, he stared at them spread out on the table. Glancing at a few of the scenery-only pictures, he slid them next to the ones of Raven. The blend was nothing short of magical.

Gull Island may be wild and rugged, beautiful and unspoiled. But it was just another Lake Superior island. What made Gull Island come to life, what made it shine with life itself, was the presence of Raven. Her connection to the island somehow breathed life into the solid chunk of rock and trees. *She* gave it life and spirit. *She* made it unique. *She* made it hers.

Leaning back in his chair, casting a quick glance at where Kizzy slept, he stared at the photos.

Absently, his fingers went to his bracelet, toying with the silver buckle. Electricity shot into his fingers, but he ignored the warnings. There seemed to be only one way he could win Raven's heart.

———

"Well, that should be everything your new pet needs for a while," Donna pointed out happily. "Now, how about another treat of tea and maybe a muffin?"

"Okay. All we need now is the vet visit for the health papers," Raven said as she followed Donna into the same little café they previously visited.

"Don't rush it. We're enjoying your visit. And we love having Sebastian home. We are in no hurry to see you two dashing off."

"That's what Sebastian said."

Donna nodded, waving to the waitress. After the orders were placed, she turned to Raven.

"Once you leave here, do you think you might return again?"

Would she? Regardless of how things worked out with Sebastian? "I might. And you two would always be welcome to visit me at Gull Island. I have plenty of room, and it is quite lovely there. Especially in the summertime."

Donna smiled, arms resting on the table. "I'm sure that is true. We might just do that one summer. I am so glad you and Sebastian worked out your issues."

Heat rushed to her cheeks. "You noticed?"

Donna reached across the table and patted her arm. "Of course we did. The tension between the two of you after the concert was so strong, it would've been impossible not to. I would also bet Diana DeLong had everything to do with it."

Raven's jaw dropped. "Why didn't you say anything?"

"Oh, honey, you and Sebastian are grown adults. It's not our place to get involved without being asked to. That woman has never been anything but trouble to Sebastian from that very first day at the awards ceremony. Fear not, Raven, he can't stand to be near her."

"That's what he said too."

"Because it's true. Raven, I can see how you still struggle with so much. Would you like my advice now?"

She brightened, sitting straighter. "Yes, of course."

Donna reached across the table to pat her arm, resting it for a moment. "Just relax and let things happen. Don't feel you have to make decisions immediately. Simply find those special moments you want to treasure forever and enjoy them for all they are worth."

That seemed like good advice. Thinking of the kisses they had shared, their bodies touching in heated passion, wishing those moments had never ended, she nodded back to Donna, blinking away the moisture building in her eyes.

———

The plane rose steadily higher. At Raven's feet, Kizzy peered through the peepholes in her airline travel bag, emitting an occasional mournful yowl. Sebastian held Raven's hand and wore a happy smile.

"Do you think she'll like living on the island?" he asked, nodding toward the kitten.

"Probably better than she liked those shots from the vet."

They shared a chuckle at how their little baby kitty had morphed into a small gray tiger when the doctor administered the required inoculations.

"Did you enjoy your visit to my hometown?"

She nodded. "I did. It was fantastic." All except the bit about Diana DeLong, but she refused to let that bother her. "I love your parents, and I like your band." She wished she had more time to get to know the guys in the band. Maybe, if she made another trip. "And I really loved your exhibit at the museum." She remembered the way his bubbling natural spring photo whispered to her. Coupled with Abby's inspirational note, she claimed it as her own.

"So you're okay with me coming back with you for a while?"

"Do you ever run out of questions?" He brought a few camera cases with him but never mentioned to her how the last ones turned out. Would he require more for the assignment, or did he habitually carry cameras whenever he traveled? He was a photographer after all.

He grinned. "Not for long." He peered at the clouds through the window. "I'll try to be better."

Right. She knew that would never last. Oh well. It was more of a running commentary between them now rather than an actual grievance.

Glancing at him during the short flight, she caught him gazing out the window, a thoughtful expression on his face, and his fingers absently rolling the leather bracelet on his wrist, fingering the stones embedded into the leather. She considered asking what he was thinking about, but instead, she touched his arm. Swinging his gaze to meet hers, she was startled to see a dampness on his lashes. Quickly, he brushed it away, giving her a lopsided smile.

Stilled by the sight, she decided not to ask what bothered him so.

Their first stop, once they landed, was to stop by the Coast Guard station. Wren wasn't in, so Raven dialed his cellphone. Sebastian grinned as she rolled her eyes at the voicemail recording.

"Hey, Wren, it's Raven. Sebastian and I are back and will be heading out to the light station as soon as we can find Ezra. Stop by when you can, or call." She looked at the carrier holding Kizzy at Sebastian's feet and nibbled her bottom lip. "I...uh...decided to add to the island's population. Talk to you later. Bye."

"That wasn't very nice. Teasing him like that."

"It's what siblings do. He'd do that to me in a heartbeat. But I do want to hear what happened when the Endeavor crash anniversary arrived and what happened to the cargo Madeline led us to."

"Me too."

It did not take long to find Ezra and arrange for him to drive them out. It was great to be back on the water again. Raven sat at the bow of the boat, wind in her face, spray tapping her cheeks as they plowed through the lake's surface. Behind her, Sebastian chatted with Ezra about boats and who had them for sale. Ahead of her, the beacon of her home flashed. Slowly, the tower came into view, then the gabled rooftop, and finally the whole house. As Ezra cut the engine, they coasted closer to the dock.

"This is it, Kizzy," she told the fur ball waiting on the boat's floor. "Your new home sweet home." Hefting the carrier and her bag, she waited as Ezra tied the boat securely.

Ezra helped them with their bags to the front door. "Stay for tea, Ezra?" she asked, once inside. "Sebastian can build some fires, and we'll get the house warmed up again."

Smiling, he accepted. He stayed long enough for one

cup of tea, plying Raven with questions about the world outside of their isolated Minnesota wooded world.

Free of her carrier, Kizzy padded softly from room to room, stealthily exploring her new surroundings. No time to play with imaginary monsters, she had serious investigating to do. Raven laughed as she crept up to each doorway and corner, ears forward, tail twitching, ready to pounce or run, depending on what she discovered next. Yes, it was good to be home again.

"Come join me in the living room," Sebastian requested once Ezra was gone, the fires built, and the teacups set aside. Taking her hand, he gently led her from the kitchen. "I have something I want to share with you."

Pulse skipping, she followed him and settled on the velvet chair by the fire.

Sebastian strode to the fire, glanced at it, heaved a sigh, and sat on the chair opposite Raven. He raked a hand through his hair.

Her lips parted in anticipation. Was this bad news?

"Sebastian," she began after he remained silent too long.

He blew out a long breath. "Okay, Raven, remember that woman on the street who thought she knew you?"

Her sharp intake halted him. He held up a hand. "Wait, I have to get this out now, so we can move on to the next big news. My big decision."

Dread settled over her as his next words fell like a hammer blow.

"Well, I, uh, know she was right because I researched you afterward."

Indignant, she stood from the chair. "You had no right to do that," she hissed. "Is nothing about me, nothing I say in confidence, sacred to you?"

"Would you have told me if I asked?" he asked quietly, watching her.

About to say yes, she slammed her mouth shut, snapping painfully. He had asked. Right then. And she refused to answer. So, of course, he had to go snooping elsewhere. Darn him. Balling her hands into fists, she marched to the window. Now he knew.

What did he do? Research her past life online and see the endless, tantalizing articles. All the horrible lies. All the mortifying photos.

Wheeling, she turned to where he waited.

"So, what did you find out, Sebastian, while you were snooping about my past?" she demanded breathlessly. "Do you feel better now that you have seen all my dirty laundry?"

Standing, he went to the fire, stuffing his hands in his back pockets, and turned to her, his shoulders hunched toward the flames. Heat boiled over within her, mixing with dread and horror.

"Damn you, answer me," she yelled. She picked up a book and flung it at him. He flinched. Sobs racked her, full of humiliation and anger. Tears blurred her vision as she grabbed a brass candlestick and released it toward him.

He bypassed it and waded in next to her. He captured her wrists and held her softly, his green gaze fixed on her.

"I found out you once owned the runways," he said softly.

CHAPTER
FOURTEEN

read about your modeling career and how great it was up until the end. I saw your pictures. They were stunning." Sebastian said, pausing. Raven stood, arms crossed, her body tense, and her lips tight. Pressing on, he drew a deep breath, going on.

"I saw the articles in the magazines and newspapers that suggested infidelity. First for you and then for him. I saw the photos of him and your best friend. Of him and other women. Curiously, I never saw any photos of you caught in the act."

"That's because I was never *in* the act," her voice rose, and her hands shot into the air. "I never, ever cheated on him!"

Holding out his hand, he tried to calm her, failing miserably. "I know that. And in time, I think others figured that out too. I also read the reports about your bitter divorce and saw more pictures of him messing around. I read about how your agents dropped you because of the stories, how your career stalled, about his short marriage to your best friend, and how you mysteriously vanished right after the divorce was finalized." He paused. "Never to be seen again."

"That's right. Until I went back to civilization *with you!*" Huffing, she marched the length of the room. Had she made it into the news headlines again? Former fashion model resurfaces—seen in Connecticut. "So now you know every single tiny morbid detail. You've seen the damning photographs. Do you feel better?"

"No, I feel worse," he admitted. "Raven, I am sorry you had to go through all that. And by the sounds of it, except for your brothers and sister, you were pretty much alone for that whole terrible experience. It must've hurt double hard to lose your best friend at the same time as your husband. I am so sorry about that."

Dropping onto a loveseat, away from his sympathetic expression, she directed a hard glare in his direction, crossing her arms across her chest. "Me too." If it had not been for Wren and Robin, and to a lesser degree Lark, she would never have survived that period. Each time she weathered the latest cold wave of disbelief, pain, and shock, they pulled her to shore as another big wave came along and ripped her out to sea again. Finally, she gave up trying to survive and wished the waves of pain and horror would suck her under for good. Only Wren and Robin stood by, holding her firmly by the lifeline of their love for her.

Unable to watch his miserable expressions anymore, and unable to listen to him anymore, she covered her ears and moved to the door. "I need some air," she stated firmly, looking back over her shoulder. "You know every embarrassing secret now. So do what you will with the information." Shrugging into her jacket, she went outside, welcoming the initial cold blast of lake air.

Bypassing the gazebo, she strolled past the light tower, following the rocky path into the meadows and the trees.

Far away, she needed to get far away. From the sympathy in his eyes and the stake he drove into her heart. She probably sounded madder than she really felt. She was more embarrassed to hear he read those damning stories, indicating she had been unfaithful when she had not been. Not even one time. He had seen photos of her on the runways, in the magazines, made up and dressed up like a queen, so far removed from how she looked these days, more like a pioneer woman of the past.

The mockery of a divorce. The shame of her best friend was exposed when she was caught in bed with her husband. That photo was almost a full page. Their staged smiles of shock. More pictures of them out on the town, not trying to hide their shame. He'd no doubt dug up all of them like a damn dog unearthing a bone. By now, he knew of her not being able to get a modeling assignment because she was, as they had called her then, too hot to handle. Tabloids followed her every move, and her husband's. And his string of women he paraded in front of them, and her, like trophies. Endless women, she had lost track of how many or where he found them. The gutters, most likely.

What had Sebastian thought of all he'd seen and read?

Memories bit at her, driving her into the woods and hills, over the crunchy, snow-packed ground. Haunting her with their derisive laughter and cruel taunts, she climbed the rocks and grabbed at tree trunks, stumbling over tangled roots, as though she were escaping pursuing demons. The demons of her past.

The trees blocked the sunshine, chilling her. Stopping to rest and catch her breath, she grasped a tree trunk, panting, and shivering.

Damn them all! Damn every single one of them! Damn them forever! Damn her ex-husband and damn her former best friend. Damn the cold. Damn the snow. Damn that woman on the street. Damn Diana DeLong. Damn the...Raven mentally paused. She ran out of things to damn and pounded the tree. Damning the tree for good measure.

Leaning her head against the tree, she slowly slid to the snowy ground. The hot tears stinging her eyes contrasted with the cold surrounding her. Tasting their saltiness, she made no move to stop them.

Clouds moved inland. She shivered against the waves of grief and confusion. She'd lost track of how much time had passed. She didn't care. Could she accept Sebastian as he was? His honest question burned her mind. Could she? Did she want to, now that there were no secrets left between them?

If he left again, and she stayed behind, it would crack her heart. Crazy, but she didn't want him to leave again. No matter how much he had upset her, she wanted him to stay. Regardless of how he could deceive with his ability, she wanted him to kiss her again. Despite all he was, she loved him.

A low growl drew her head up. Sniffing the tears away, she searched the woods and shadows. A dark form lumbered into view, flanked by towering pines. A bear glared at her with lips curled in a hideous grimace.

Gasping, she dragged herself upright and stared at the black bear. Didn't they usually hibernate by now? She thought they did. Had she ever encountered a bear this time of year? Not that she recalled. Heart thudding, she gripped the tree.

Grunting, the beast smelled the air, shaking its big, shaggy head at her.

Legs shaking, she searched for an escape. She was much further into the hills than normal. The house and tower were far, far below. She would never stand a chance if she were to run.

Unless...

"That better not be you, Sebastian Knight," she said to the bear. Standing tall, she took a step away from the tree, with a hand gripping the bark. "Because if that is you, I am not impressed."

The bear growled once, raising a front paw, as if to swing out.

"There is no need for this. If that's really you."

The bear lumbered a step closer, listening to her defiant voice. Lips curled back, nose twitching, he smelled the air.

"Damn you. I had just about made up my mind that I wanted you to stay. Now, if you're going to do something stupid like this, I'm not so sure."

The bear rose to its hind feet. His huge claws raked the air. A mighty growl filled the air.

"Sebastian?" Her whispered voice broke as she fell against the tree. "That isn't you, is it?"

———

Sebastian sat at the table, spinning the bracelet around his wrist. Her past tore at his heart, her pain refreshed by his bringing it up. Did he really have to do that? Go where he knew he would hit the nerves, where the sharpest thorns were? He thought he had been honest with her, but now the doubts about his decision poked him. He thought he had to get that all out to build an honest future. Had he been wrong? Well, it's too late now. The words were spoken. And so was she. Running around out there, hurting again.

He had wanted to move on to his next step, his big declaration. His ultimate decision. Now he doubted he'd get the chance. She was likely to send him off with Ezra the moment she got back. A sigh escaped him, like a tire going flat. Would he ever be able to prune her prickly thorns without hurting them both in the process?

Fingering the stones, feeling the heat inside them, he paused. She was worth it. She was worth anything to him. He was going to do this. Heart thudding, he sucked in a breath.

Reaching for the silver buckle, he winced at the hot, electric jolts of warning stabbing his fingers. The magic. Somehow, the bracelet knew his intentions.

For Raven, he reminded himself, pushing the leather strap up and ignoring the fiery heat. Sucking in a breath, he prepared himself, like ripping off a bandage. A very hot, scorching bandage.

Madeline materializing suddenly at his side, standing inches away as a white apparition, made him jump, hand over his heart.

"Madeline!" he yelped. "You about scared me to...well, badly."

Eying the ghostly girl, he expected her to fade away now that she'd scared him witless. Leave him alone to do the deed. Remove the bracelet and forever be only a man. Raven's man, he hoped.

Madeline, face somber, hovered, staring at him, her hand reaching out.

Come now.

Sebastian heard the words as clearly as if Madeline had spoken them aloud.

Climbing to his feet, aware of the sizzle on his wrist as he pushed the strap back in place, he grabbed his coat next. Madeline passed through the door. Fear lodged in his chest. He yanked the door open and met her in the cold air.

She led him wordlessly down the path, glancing over her shoulder as if to ensure he was still following her. Heart thumping, straining his ears, he heard nothing more than the water washing ashore and the wind blowing through the treetops overhead. Looking at the lake, the water was unusually calm. The surface was like black ice, mirroring the trees along the shore.

Madeline floated quickly through the woods, into the hills, passing through trees and over tangled branches.

Stumbling through the snow, downed logs, and roots, he struggled to keep up with her, no match for her spiritual speed. Branches slapped him as he gamely tried to keep up with her pace. Where was Madeline leading him? His stomach twisted into hard knots. Raven was at the end of this quest.

Breaking into a stand of trees, deep snarls reverberate in his ears before the black bear came into view. It stood on its hind feet, waving its front clawed paws in the air. Swallowing hard, he followed Madeline's pointing finger to Raven, huddled against a tree.

Oh God. Going cold all over, the bracelet sizzled. His teeth lengthened, his nose broadened, and his hands and nails expanded. Emitting a mighty roar, he charged the other bear, slamming his shaggy shoulder against the other bear's shoulder.

Dodging nimbly out of the way, he narrowly missed a powerful swat with the claws. Spinning, he rose to his hind feet, growling, showing all his teeth and fangs. The bear stepped forward, wrapping its arms around him, teeth going for his throat. Wrapping his arms around the bear, almost gagging on its horrible breath, he attempted to push it away.

Standing head-to-head, chest to chest, they pushed and pulled, snarling and growling, jaws snapping. His injured arm took a beating, but the adrenaline rush of matching the bear in a protective fury for Raven overpowered the pain.

Twigs and small trees broke under their weight as they stomped through the snow. The black bear dragged Sebastian down to all fours. The bear's teeth grabbed the fur around his neck, narrowly missing the leather collar of his bracelet nestled next to his skin.

Sebastian slid from under the brute. Whirling around, he slammed his head into the other bear's chest and grabbed its massive leg in his mouth.

A mighty slap from the beast's paw had him rolling through the snow. Landing hard against a stout tree, he sat on his haunches. Sitting a moment to clear his mind, he watched as the black bear lumbered closer.

He inhaled the rank fur. As he felt its hot breath on him, he brought his front paws up and held them away like cymbals. Then, with a matching growl, he brought them forward and crashed them with all his bear-strength might on both sides of the bear's skull.

Dazed, the black bear halted, dropped to its rear, and stared blindly at Sebastian. Sebastian gave a mighty roar, baring his teeth. The black bear staggered to its feet and bounded over the hill.

Limping to where he left his clothes, he shifted into himself, hastily pulling on the garments. Breathless, he cast a wary glance at Raven, still rooted by the tree, wide-eyed and mouth agape.

"Are you okay?" he asked, adjusting the bandage over his arm again. Which might need some attention. But later.

———

Wordlessly, Raven nodded, not moving from her post. Despite having seen him shift before, it still left her, well, it left her a whole lot of things. Stunned. Amazed. Speechless. She had watched as he dressed, and as he pulled his coat on, he took a tentative step toward her, a wariness in his eyes.

"Are you alright?" she asked, voice barely above a whisper. "Your arm?"

"It's good enough for now. I'll have a headache though. That bear could pack a wallop." He offered her a grin, not quite reaching his eyes. He stopped several feet from her, hands going into his pockets.

"How did you know? Animal intuition?"

"No, Madeline came and told me." He searched the area before returning to her. "She's getting to be handy to have around. Next time I see her, I owe her a thank you."

Apparently, she did too. How had Madeline known about the bear?

"Look, Raven," he began, advancing. He took her hands into his, looking deep into her eyes. She shifted under the intense scrutiny. "That is going to be the last time you see me shift. I," he paused, swallowing, "I'm taking the bracelet off."

"No!" A shocked gasp escaped her. "Wait. You're willing to do that? For me?"

He nodded, giving her a little grin. "Crazy Arthur was right after all. There is plenty of treasure here on Gull Island. And I found mine. Raven Koynes, you are all the treasure I want and need."

Darn him, but the heat flooded her cheeks, warming her body. Heart skipping, she gazed into his eyes, drinking him in as hot tears built in her eyes. She blinked away the wetness and pulled her hands free, bringing them to rest on his waist. Twice, she's witnessed his shifting. Both times were to save her. And his guise as Salzburg had been the same, protecting her the only way he could.

"I can't let you take the bracelet off," she said softly, smiling at the slow confusion growing on his face. "Your ability is as much a part of you as your eyes, height, or anything else. Your endless questions." She laughed, looping her fingertips through the narrow space of the bracelet. The leather was worn soft and warm from his skin. "Changing who you are would be wrong. Maybe I needed to see its beauty in order to appreciate its uniqueness." She pulled him closer. "And it's beautiful when it is done through love."

He tilted his head. A slow smile grew on his face. He cupped her chin, bringing her to touch him. Hot desire knifed through her as he parted her lips, probing her mouth and then delivering a bold kiss.

Liquid heat spread over her like wildfire and met his fiery demand. Standing on tiptoes to reach him, her hands stretched up to grab his shirt. His musky scent filled her nose. Now she understood it was his natural animal magic and not a cologne.

She broke the kiss and took his hands to her waist. She pressed him closer until there was no space between them.

"I never want anything between us." She spoke. "Not secrets. Not anything."

"Agreed, my darling."

Sebastian's caress of her hair was pure magic.

EPILOGUE

Raven sat in the swing Sebastian had constructed and hung for her. From this tree, she could watch out over the water, counting the waves, or turn around and watch the house. Seagulls cried and flapped their wings overhead, dipping to the water. Kicking a little higher, she idly counted the gulls and the waves, waiting.

She gazed toward where Sebastian had said the *Endeavor* rested under the waves. Wren gave them an update about the stakeout at Madeline's cave. Two days later, a boat with six men arrived, planning to pick up the lost cargo. Immediately arrested, Wren said it didn't take long for them to spill their secrets.

The *Endeavor's* sinking was an accident. But the house that was supposed to take custody of the items had some unsavory high-ranking members of the board. They cooked up a scheme to have divers move the shipping crates inland to a safe place where they could be stored while the insurance company investigated and ultimately paid out for the loss. Then, once the incident died out, buried in rumors and speculation, they could reclaim the lost artifacts and sell them on the black market at a huge profit.

Now their only profits were lost jobs and long prison sentences. The Coast Guard was holding custody of the entire cargo until proper ownership could be settled.

It was fascinating, and Raven wondered how Madeline knew where the cave and cargo were. More importantly, she wondered where Sebastian was. She checked the time on her watch. Almost four-fifteen.

Sebastian had said he expected to be back by four with the boat he was buying. Since he was staying on at the light station, now that they were officially married, he needed a boat to get them to the mainland and the Coast Guard station occasionally. He and Wren had become fast friends. She wasn't arguing about either one. Once the baby arrived, she would certainly want ready transportation.

Patting her belly, starting to swell with child, she smiled. Their baby. Due in another five months. Would he or she have Sebastian's shapeshifting ability? He had said he doubted it but wasn't sure. She dared not hope either way.

Robin and Ricky had their baby, Hannah Grace, who was now three months old. Twice, she and Sebastian visited them. And Sebastian's parents promised to come back and visit once the baby was born. They had fallen in love with the Victorian charm of the house when they came for the wedding.

And the best gift of all? Sebastian had only sent six photos of Gull Island for his assignment. Two from his stormy ride on the lake, one from atop the light tower, shot at the height of the painted skies, and three from up in the hills. While showcasing the beauty of Gull Island they did nothing to make it stand out as a tourist destination. Instead, they showed it to be just another rugged and isolated Lake Superior Island. Nothing special, nothing unique.

Due to the insistence of Sebastian's parents, she was

toying with the possibility of displaying some of her paintings alongside his works in select galleries. She insisted that they would be unnamed, making no reference to Gull Island. That way, no one would eagerly look it up on a map and start a trend. After all, they needed to protect their island sanctuary now more than ever.

She smiled, thinking of how well their secret was protected. Gull Island was special; it was home to one teenage ghost, one shapeshifter, two people madly in love, and soon to be home to a wonderful little baby. Shapeshifting ability or not, their baby was going to be wonderful.

And they both hoped the baby would be joined by lots of brothers and sisters in the years to come. Sebastian had said he liked the history of how the old light keepers had large families, and he wanted to keep the tradition alive. And she wasn't complaining.

He'd also read parts of Madeline's journal and her mother's. They both agreed that the entries helped them understand Madeline better, as well as the sometimes hard and lonely life early lightkeepers and their families lived while on the island. And the tragedies that could happen.

A boat's horn brought her back to reality. She watched a sleek, blue and white motorboat putter alongside the dock. Sebastian waved, wearing an enormous, happy smile.

Waving, she brought the swing to a halt, smiling as she crossed the rocks to meet him. Her husband was home.

THANK YOU FOR READING

———

Did you enjoy this book?

We invite you to leave a review at your favorite book site, such as Goodreads, Amazon, Barnes & Noble, etc.

DID YOU KNOW THAT LEAVING A REVIEW...

- Helps other readers find books they may enjoy.
- Gives you a chance to let your voice be heard.
- Gives authors recognition for their hard work.
- Doesn't have to be long. A sentence or two about why you liked the book will do.

ABOUT THE AUTHOR

 Ryan Jo Summers lives in North Carolina. Her first published non-fiction came in 2007 with articles for local, and eventually national magazines. In 2012 she released her first fiction novel. Since then, she has released countless articles and over two dozen novels and novellas with assorted publishers. She also released two self-published books. Her style in fiction writing would broadly be labeled as clean, sweet romance. Many of her works have been nominated and placed in national writing contests.

Ryan Jo's other passion beyond writing is animals. She has worked as a veterinary technician, director in a non-profit rescue shelter, provided foster care, and more recently she worked as a dog walker and boarding service. She has a menagerie of rescued pets who keep her company and offer inspiration. While she lives land-locked, she dreams of packing up her dogs and going to the beach.

Website: www.ryanjosummers.com
Blog: summersrye.wordpress.com
Facebook: www.facebook.com/RyanJoSummersAuthor

 facebook.com/RyanJoSummersAuthor

ALSO BY RYAN JO SUMMERS

WITH SATIN ROMANCE

Novels/Novellas

Glimpse Eternity

It Happened at the Park

Wild Whispers

Chasing Painted Skies

Holiday Romance

Magic in the Snow

Christmas at Crazy Woman Creek

Anthologies

Coffeecake Chaos in Food & Romance Go Together Vol. 1